# Touching the Dead

A Jo Wolfe psychic detective thriller

Wendy Cartmell

This kindle edition published 2020
Costa Press

ISBN: 9798626152661

# By Wendy Cartmell

**Sgt Major Crane crime thrillers**
Deadly Steps
Deadly Nights
Deadly Honour
Deadly Lies
Deadly Widow
Hijack
Deadly Cut
Deadly Proof

**Emma Harrison Mysteries**
Past Judgement
Mortal Judgement
Joint Judgement

**Crane and Anderson crime thrillers**
Death Rites
Death Elements
Death Call
A Grave Death
A Cold Death

**Supernatural Mysteries**
Gamble with Death
Touching the Dead
Divining the Dead
Watching the Dead

For Ben
whose unusual gift inspired this series.
Thank you!

.

# 1

The cold wind whipped her black hair over her face, as DI Jo Wolfe climbed out of the car with little enthusiasm. A windswept bank at Bosham wasn't the best place to be on a wintery early morning. She stopped at the boot of her car, a bright red Mini Clubman, the only thing of colour in the bleached landscape. After exchanging her shoes for wellingtons and tucking her trousers into them, she swapped her woollen tweed coat for her waterproof Barbour and followed her colleague, DS Byrd, out of the car park.

'Come on, Guv, keep up!' he shouted.

'Why? The body isn't going anywhere!'

As she slid through the mud, Jo acknowledged she was in a terrible mood, exacerbated by the amount of vodka she'd drunk the night before and the lateness of the hour hitting her bed. It was all her bloody father's fault. He was retired and didn't have to get up for work in the morning, like she had to. He was a bad influence. She smiled at the irony. Normally it was the child behaving badly, not the parent.

She called out to Byrd to wait for her, but her words were snatched away by the wind. She saw him greet a couple of uniformed officers who were pointing the way to the body as she caught up with him.

'It's just round that bend, Guv,' and Byrd strode off again.

'It?' Jo struggled to keep up with him as she slid on the wet ground, feeling as though she were on a fairground ride, one of the ones where the floor kept moving. Haunted house. Fun house. Something like that.

'The body.'

'I know that, but it's male or female, not a bloody it. Really, Byrd, you know better than that,' Jo grumbled.

'We don't know yet.'

'What?'

'If its male or female.'

'Why the hell not?'

'That's why,' and Byrd indicated what at first glance appeared to be a load of dirty rags on the bank of the Chichester Harbour.

As Jo got closer, she realised what Byrd meant.

'Jesus,' she said, pulling her hair out of her eyes. 'Are those bandages? It looks like a mummy. Is it Halloween and someone forgot to tell me?'

'Yes they are, yes it does and no it isn't.'

'Alright, Byrd, cut the wise cracks. What do we know?' She squatted down to take a closer look.

'Not much. A dog walker found the body, if it is a body, about 30 minutes ago. He was walking along, throwing sticks for his Labrador, when the dog made a bee line for what he thought was a pile of rags. He called the dog back and went to look. He said the dog didn't do any damage, only had a good sniff. But his master couldn't hold onto his breakfast and he threw up in the scrub, over there. He's waiting back at the car park. A tent is being brought down to preserve the scene, and forensics and the pathologist are on their way.'

'I don't think the scene will be able to tell us much,' Jo said, looking around the bank. 'By the mud on the wrappings it looks as though she may have been buried in a shallow grave and the tidal water has washed the top layer of soil away. And the water will no doubt have destroyed any evidence.'

Byrd nodded his agreement. 'Our only hope is that there may be something we can use on the body or on the underlying layers of bandages.'

Jo straightened as officers arrived with a white plastic tent to preserve the scene and moved out of their way.

'Right, back to the car then. You can go and get some coffees and I'll wait for Bill and Jeremy.'

Byrd looked as though he was going to moan, but kept his mouth shut at a glare from Jo. As she followed her DS back to her car, she ran through her core team: herself DI Jo Wolfe, her partner DS Eddie Byrd, forensic specialist Bill Burke and back at the office, team manager Judith Thompson. The pathologist should be Jeremy Grogan. She needed to make sure her boss, DCI Alex Crooks, gave her the case and she reached for her mobile to phone him.

She woke a sleepy DCI who didn't seem very pleased to hear from her.

'Jesus, Jo, it's my day off. What the hell do you want?'

'Caught a new case, Boss. Dead body found down in Bosham. I'm there now.'

'So?'

'So it looks as though the body has been mummified.'

'What?' Jo heard bed clothes rustling and springs creaking. 'Mummified?'

'Yes, that's what I said. Interesting, eh?'

'Very. I'm on my way.'

'Really? I only wanted permission to take the case and pick the team.'

'Take that as read, Jo. This one's too good to pass on. I'll be there soon. It'll be worth looking in-situ.'

Jo was left holding a dead phone, a wry grin on her face as she thought about Crooks' enthusiasm for the case, which matched her own. Her Major Crimes unit were the brightest and finest in the Sussex police. They got the best, or worst cases, depending on your point of view. The brass definitely used her for the nasty cases. Sometimes they made the headlines, sometimes not. If the public knew what really went on, if they knew about the close shaves and the gruesome murders, well they might not sleep well at night.

But maybe they would, knowing Jo Wolfe was on the case.

The haunting call of seagulls brought her back to the present and she got into the car to wait for Byrd to come back with a comforting hot coffee. She looked over the water, which glistened in the weak winter sunlight and realised what an isolated place the burial site was. If it wasn't for the recent storms, the body would have lain undisturbed, lonely and forgotten, possibly forever. Out there somewhere was a grieving family and it was Jo's job to give them answers and give the victim a decent burial and peaceful rest. And to catch the depraved murderer who'd done it. There was no doubt in Jo's mind that it was murder, after all wrapping dead bodies in bandages was not a common practice in the UK. Nor would someone wrap themselves in bandages, dig a grave, then pop themselves in it and wait to die.

It would be interesting to find out what lay beneath the bandages. What the body would be able to forensically tell them about the perpetrator and the victim, if anything. And then finally what it would be able to tell her. Jo would get her chance to touch the dead girl in due course. But for now, she needed to be patient and wait for the post-mortem.

Tyres crunching on the gravel broke through her reverie and made Jo look up. She grinned as Byrd led a convoy of vehicles into the car park, her bad mood and hangover quite forgotten.

## 2

Back at the inauspicious Chichester police station, a 1970's building with no character and quite possibly no longer fit for purpose, Jo and her team were bringing each other up to date with the case so far. She was frustrated already. It was late afternoon and there was still no identification of the body, which meant no impetus to the investigation. Their boss had met them at the burial site, but he hadn't been able to add anything to the investigation, apart from saying that he'd never seen anything like it. He then left them to it and went home to his wife to enjoy a cooked breakfast. Jo and Byrd had wondered how he could eat after seeing a mummified body, but each to their own.

'When is the post-mortem?' Jo asked Byrd.

'Jeremy said around 10 am tomorrow. He's pretty backed up, what with a fatal car crash and a suspicious death in an old people's home. But he's prioritised this one for us, Guv.'

'Thanks, Byrd. Until then, when the bandages will come off, there's not much we can do about identification. I take it we still don't know definitively if the body is that of a male or female?'

'No, sorry, but it's looking more like it's a female, given the you know what's,' and Byrd made a motion with his hands indicating breasts.

'Alright, Byrd, we get the picture. Bill?'

Burke said, as he smoothed down his beard, 'As you suspected, Guv, there was little we could get from the scene. There was just mud, mud and more mud. No footprints, tyre tracks, shovel marks. The mud was as smooth as a baby's bum thanks to the tidal water. We're hopeful we can get something from the PM, after which we'll get access to the bandages and anything found on the body. Sorry, Guv, there's not much I can do in the meantime.' He rubbed his bald head as if in frustration.

Jo had the same feeling of impotence. 'Has anyone got good news for me?'

'I might, Guv.'

'Thank goodness. Go on, Judith.'

Judith tucked her pen behind her ear, where it kept her muddy coloured straight hair off her face. 'If we look at the picture as a whole, we've got, mummification, body found on the bank of a body of water and placed in a shallow grave. Those three elements together could be an indication of Egyptian tradition.'

'Egyptian? Why the hell would Egypt have anything to do with our dead body?'

'I can't answer the why, but I'm pretty sure about the what.'

'That's interesting,' Jo mused. Then deciding to run with it said, 'Can you do some more research on that, Judith? The only thing I know about Egypt is that stupid song, "Walk like an Egyptian" by the Bangles and the lyrics never made much sense to me.'

'What about an Egyptologist?' said Byrd.

'Nice,' agreed Judith.

Jo nodded. 'Find one, Judith.'

'Will do, Ma'am.'

Judith coloured as Jo glared at her. 'Sorry, Guv. My mistake.'

Jo hated being called Ma'am. It might be a sign of respect for her rank, but as far as she was concerned it was an old fashioned, outdated form of address. She much preferred being called Guv or Boss.

'Right, there's clearly not much else we can do today. Wrap it up and head off home for a good night's sleep. It may be the last opportunity we get in a while.'

Chairs scraped and laptops closed as Jo walked to the wall. All they had were pictures of the mummified body in situ, an enlarged map of the area where it was found and a whole load of questions. She shook her head in frustration. The beginning of a headache made her rub her temples. Her fingers traced the knobbly scar on the right one. She then reached up to release her hair from its clip. Shaking her head and pulling her fingers through the resultant mess eased the strain on her forehead, but not the headache. Involuntarily, her fingers caught the scar on the top of her head. There was no pain there anymore, but the accident and then the coma had left her with blinding migraine headaches when she became stressed. She knew she had to look after herself, ease back off the gas when she could. She still had days when she felt weak and fatigued, but they were infrequent, several years on from the accident. There was nothing else for it. She should go home as well.

Driving to the house in Boxgrove that she shared with her father, she pondered the act of mummifying a body. Was it because someone was enamoured with Egypt and its history and was following their practices? If so, why? What was the fascination? Where did it come from? She hoped Judith would be able to find a specialist who could come and talk to them tomorrow afternoon. In the meantime she'd do a google search.

As she entered the sleepy village, she slowed the speed of her Mini Clubman until she got to the family home. Located on the edge of the village, she lived in a three bedroomed detached house with a two bedroomed granny annex over the garages, which she owned with her father. As she pulled up in front of their home, he opened the door.

'Thought that was you,' he called. 'How's it going?'

Himself a retired DI, her father was always interested in her cases and he'd want to know about the new one. She'd told him she had a new case when he'd rung earlier in the day to talk to her about a family get-together he wanted her to attend.

'Slowly, Dad,' Jo said. 'Give me 10 then come over. I'll put the kettle on.'

Mick Wolfe gave Jo a thumbs up and she climbed the stairs to her flat above the garage block. To some it might be a topsy-turvy arrangement, dad in the house and her in the granny annex, but it was a neat, flipped pact that suited them both. Her siblings could come and go, visiting dad and leaving Jo in peace when she was on a case, or just hating the world and needing to shut herself away.

She quickly changed into sweats and put the kettle on. She heard her father's footsteps on the stairs just as she was pinning photographs of the mummified body onto her wall, which would replicate the one in her office as the investigation progressed.

Her father was studying the pictures as she made the tea and then gave him a mug.

'What do you think?' she asked.

'Bloody interesting.'

'I thought you'd say that.'

'Have you had a chance to be with the body yet?'

'No. It won't be until after the post-mortem tomorrow.'

Jo rubbed her temples yet again. She was losing her battle with the headache.

She watched Mick study the photos. He was dressed in sweats, as she was. His black hair was gathering grey ones at a rapid pace and his face was alive with wrinkles. She always teased that he was a dinosaur. An old-school detective, who'd joined the police force before the days of computerised records, in the year dot. Jo was part of the new generation attracted to the police force. She went to university obtaining a degree in criminology and forensic psychology, and after a couple of years working, she then joined the service via the Police Now programme and became a detective. She was the only one of his three children that had followed their father into the service. Together they were a mix of the old and the new. He was her go-to guy when she was stressed, obsessed or stuck on a case.

But, of course, no one could know she was sharing her cases with him. Nor about her unique gift.

It was their secret and she intended to keep it that way.

# 3

Jo's priority the next morning was the post-mortem of the mummified body and Jo and Eddie were at the mortuary at Chichester General Hospital in plenty of time, both in their usual work attire of a dark suit. Jo always wore trousers and most of the time flat shoes or trainers. She viewed any other clothing or footwear as impractical for her job. Neither did she carry a handbag, using pockets for her badge, notebook and keys.

They watched from the observation deck as Jeremy Grogan started. Dressed in scrubs with gloved hands, an apron on and a cap over his blond hair, he dictated what he saw before him; a body wrapped in bandages taken out of a muddy grave yesterday. The first thing he'd done was an x-ray of the whole mummy. That had indicated there was indeed a body under the bandages, but nothing else that could help them, such as a knife or a gun. Neither were there any bullets in any part of the body.

Tendrils of bandage sprouted from various parts of the corpse and dripped muddy water onto the table and the floor.

Jeremy mused aloud. 'Should I cut the bandages away, or unwrap them?'

'Will you be able to unwrap them, without damaging the body which you'll have to lift up and down as the bandages unwind?'

'Good point, Jo.' Jeremy turned to look up at her. 'If I cut them up the middle of the torso, I might be able to free the chest that way and then possibly unwind the face, arms and legs. I'll start on the head and see how it goes.'

Jeremy made sure the head was raised on a neck block and grabbed a loose piece of bandage. As it was unwound, the first thing Jo and Byrd saw was black hair. Then the face, which was chalk white with purple lips. Eyes open, mouth open in silent scream. It looked like a female and one that had died in agony. Jeremy collected the bandages taken from the head and they were placed in an evidence bag.

'I think this is going to be a bad one, Byrd.'

'So do I, Boss,' and Jo watched Eddie close his eyes and grip the railing, swaying slightly as though feeling faint.

'You alright?'

Byrd nodded in agreement, but Jo wasn't convinced. It really was a troubling sight. That poor girl, Jo thought. What on earth had happened to her to make her look like a pastiche of the Edvard Munch painting, "The Scream"?

They soon found out.

Jeremy easily cut away the bandages on the torso and was able to open them outwards, enabling them to see the chest cavity. The chest cavity? Shit.

'Jeremy, what's going on?' Jo heard her voice wobble in horror.

'Um, it appears the victim has undergone some kind of surgery.'

'What the hell does that mean?' Jo was peering down at the victim, trying to make some sense of the mangled mess of flesh and bone on display.

'It would appear the skin has been cut, peeled away from the chest and then the ribs broken to give access to the chest cavity. Just like the procedure in an autopsy.'

'How vile, but how did she die?'

'I'd say because of her heart.'

'Oh, did she have a heart attack?'

'No, it was taken out. And by the looks of things, the procedure was started while the victim was still alive.'

'Jesus Christ,' whispered Byrd.

'So where the hell is her heart?'

'Hey, don't shoot the messenger! That's for you to find out, Jo.'


Once the autopsy was complete, Jo and Byrd left the mortuary and retired to a local café for copious amounts of caffeine to try to help them put the horror of the state of the body into perspective, before going back to the office. Jo soon realised that it was a pointless exercise. Nothing helped.

'Who the hell could do that to another human being?' a rhetorical question, knowing that Eddie had no more idea than she had. 'I know we tend to have the nasty, horrible cases, but I don't think any of us have come across anything so inhumane.'

'It makes me bloody angry, Jo.'

She nodded in reply, not minding that Eddie used her first name, as was his habit when they were on their own. 'Me too.'

'So we need to channel that.'

'Absolutely,' she agreed.

'We will catch him.' Eddie banged on the café table

to emphasise his point, then realised his mistake as the other customers looked round at them.

Jo nodded and covered his clenched fist with her hand. 'You're right, Eddie. We need to be positive to counteract all the adversity that we're going to meet in this case. It's not going to be an easy one.'

'There's so little to go on,' he grumbled.

'At the moment, yes,' said Jo and retrieved her hand as she realised she was still gripping his. 'But we'll gather more information, create leads, you know how it works, slowly, slowly does it.'

'Let's hope not too bloody slowly. He might strike again.'

'He?'

'He? Her? Who knows?' Then Byrd smiled at Jo. 'Come on then, let's get to it.'

'You go on ahead,' Jo said. 'I'll be there shortly. There's just one more thing I have to do.'

'Okay, you're the boss,' and Byrd tossed her the car keys. 'See you back at the ranch.'

4

Jo made her way back to the mortuary as Jeremy was just leaving the suite.

'You alright, Jo?'

'Yes, sure, I just wanted a few minutes with our victim.'

'Be my guest,' and he walked over to the cold storage, checked a label and then pulled open the drawer. 'Take as long as you want.'

Joining him, Jo said, 'Thanks, Jeremy,' and then waited until he'd politely left the room.

Jo folded down the linen that covered their victim's face. Then looking down at the poor girl whose dark hair made her alabaster skin appear even whiter, Jo stroked her head.

'I want to help you,' she whispered. 'Let me help find your killer. Show me what happened.'

Jo slipped her hand into the girl's and held it, putting her other hand over it, so it was sandwiched between them.

Then she waited.

*The flash rocked Jo back on her heels, even though she'd been expecting it and she tightened her grip on the victim.*

*'No, please no, don't, please! HELP! Someone help me! I DON'T WANT TO DIE! Why are you doing this? Why me?'*

*The hairs on the back of Jo's neck stood up as she heard and felt the girl's fear. It permeated every bone in her body. Every fibre. Every cell. The girl had never been so afraid in all her life. And to be honest, neither had Jo.*

*'Because you're a slut, a whore, a SINNER!' The deep, booming voice filled Jo's head. 'You will be judged and found wanting.'*

*Jo began shaking but was determined to keep a hold of the girl's hand. This was the most powerful reading she'd ever had, and it made her sick to her stomach.*

*The stench of evil filled Jo's nostrils and she began to take small, shallow breaths through her mouth. Panting, just like the dead girl before her had done.*

*The heat began to drain from Jo's body, as she became as cold as the girl being tortured. She shivered.*

*Then with a tremendous force of will, Jo opened her eyes, and for just a moment she was able to see what the victim saw.*

*The mortuary disappeared and if anyone had been there to witness what Jo was doing, they would have seen the blankness in her eyes. Jo was looking at something other. The colour of her pupils faded away as the darkness took her.*

*The girl was spread eagled on a metal table. She was naked and tied down at the wrists and ankles. Cold, so cold. She appeared to be in an underground chamber. Brick walls, dirt floor, no windows. She couldn't see much else, as her head was pinned down as well. The overall impression was of a crumbling, abandoned space.*

*Then she saw an animal looming over her. A horse? No, not that big. A dog? No bigger. A wolf? That was it. Grinning. Mouth open to reveal rows of sharp white teeth. Big, bad wolf.*

*Jo opened her mouth and from it poured a silent scream.*

*The girl thrashed against the bindings tying her to the table and began begging for the wolf not to hurt her and to let her go.*

*And then the connection was lost.*

Jo let go of the dead girl's hand. She was weak and shaking and held onto the drawer as she was in danger of collapse. It took a while before Jo was composed enough to be able to stand up unaided. Her right temple throbbed, and she passed her fingers over the raised scar, rubbing it.

As she slid the drawer inward, Jo promised the victim that whoever this lunatic was, big, bad wolf, she would do everything in her power to find him and bring him to justice.

# 5

Back at the office, Byrd was pinning up the photos that had been taken at the post-mortem that morning.

'Don't put the chest cavity ones up, Byrd,' Jo said as she walked out of her office.

'Too gruesome?'

'For the moment, just because Judith's Egyptian bloke is on his way.'

'Got it,' said Byrd and put those photos in his desk drawer, just as they heard voices and Judith appeared with a man in tow.

'Professor Russell, our boss, Jo Wolfe and this is Detective Sgt Eddie Byrd. Bill Burke is away in the lab, but we'll fill him in later.'

Russell approached Jo with his hand out. She took it and he placed his other hand over hers, sandwiching it. A politician's handshake. She saw a flash in his eyes as he smiled at her, which unsettled Jo. Was he flirting with her? Maybe it was just that surrounded with nubile young women every day at the university, he considered himself a player and that every attractive woman was fair game.

*Big, bad, wolf.*

Jo was shaken and pulled her hand away. Where the hell had that come from? And what, if anything, did it mean? Was it just a memory from seeing their victim that resurfaced in her mind? Or was it something more? A message? A warning?

Judith found the professor a seat and the three officers lounged where they were, sitting on office chairs and on the edge of desks. Jo's hand was still tingling from the encounter and she was trying hard not to show how much the handshake had affected her. She cleared her throat and then picked up her mug of coffee, hiding behind the prop.

'Thanks for coming, Professor, it's appreciated,' said Judith.

'Glad to help,' Russell said as a lock of black hair fell over his forehead. He sported a popular haircut of short at the back and sides and longer on top. 'May I study the photos?'

'Of course, help yourself,' said Jo and pointed to the boards.

Once he'd looked at the photos on the wall and returned to his chair he said, 'So what do you want from me?'

Jo said, 'Do you think our case has any elements of Egyptian practices.'

'One question first.'

'Yes?'

'How did she die?'

'Her chest was opened, and her heart cut out.'

Jo's brutal words had the effect she wanted, and Russell closed his eyes for a moment. Then he said, 'That's what I expected you to say. Therefore, there's no doubt in my mind that it does.'

Into the silence that followed, Byrd spoke. 'Where are you based, Professor? I hope we've not dragged you too far from home.'

Jo thought Byrd was trying to be nice to the poor man after her bluntness.

'I've only come from Chichester University,' said Professor Russell, 'so it wasn't any bother at all. In fact I must admit to being rather captivated by your investigation.'

'Really?'

'Yes.' Russell took his jacket off and rolled up his shirtsleeves. Jo wondered if he was planning on staying a long time. She hoped not. 'Sorry it's so hot in here,' she said. 'The heating is on the blink and it's got stuck at 'rainforest' temperature.'

He smiled and Jo noticed he had twinkling blue eyes, which she immediately avoided. But she had to admit that under his trendy slim fitting button down collar shirt and jeans that were obviously Levi's, he had quite a body for a man in what? His late 30's?

Byrd said, 'What are your initial thoughts, Professor?'

'Well, based upon what we know so far - the mummification of the body and taking out of the heart - it could be the work of the God of Death.'

Judith said, 'I beg your pardon?' She'd gone as white as the Professor's shirt.

'Who the hell is that?' growled Jo, not liking what she was hearing.

'Anubis. Here's a picture.'

He flicked through his document folder, then stood up and pinned a picture to the board so they could all see it.

'Bloody hell he's got a wolf's head on,' exclaimed Byrd.

'Did he wear a real one, do you think?' said Judith and shivered.

'Big, bad, wolf,' mumbled Jo, more to herself than the room, as she felt the world tip on its axis. The picture on the board was too similar to what she'd seen in the vision for it to be anything else.

Byrd heard her. 'Sorry, Boss?'

She shook her head, 'Nothing.'

'His name is Anubis,' said the Professor. 'Readings of the hieroglyphics say that someone had to protect the dead, because a common problem was the digging up of bodies shortly after burial, by jackals and wild dogs. So Anubis became a protector of graves and cemeteries. The dead were usually buried on the west bank of the Nile.'

'But why would he do this to her?' Byrd got the photo of the open, empty chest cavity from his drawer and handed it to the Professor.

Professor Russell baulked at the photo, then closed his eyes and took a minute to regain his composure. 'I believe it's to do with the Judgement of the Dead. Let me explain,' he leaned forward, elbows on his knees. 'To the Ancient Egyptians, the judgement of the dead was the process that allowed the gods to judge the worthiness of the souls of the deceased. Deeply rooted in the Egyptian belief of immortality, judgement was one of the most important parts of the journey through the afterlife.

'Once the deceased finished their journey through the underworld, they arrived at the Hall of Maat. There their purity would be the determining factor in whether they would be allowed to enter the Kingdom of Osiris. After confirming that they were sinless, the deceased was presented with the balance that was used to weigh their heart against the feather of Maat. Anubis was the god often seen administering this test.'

'Test? asked Judith. 'What test?'

'If the deceased's heart balanced with the feather of Maat, Thoth would record the result and they would be presented to Osiris, who admitted them into the

Sekhet-Aaru. A bit like our heaven. However, if their heart was heavier than the feather, it was to be devoured by the Goddess Ammit, permanently destroying the soul of the deceased.'

No one spoke. Jo didn't think any of them were capable of speech at that moment. Her head was swimming with pictures of Anubis with a wolf's head on, dressed in Egyptian clothing, hearts being torn out of chests and the connection with her surname. Each one made her shudder anew.

'Sorry,' mumbled a white-faced Judith, as she rushed out of the office.

'That means,' Byrd stopped and coughed, before starting again. 'That means he is going to kill again.'

'I would say it's highly likely,' confirmed Professor Russell.

'Big, bad wolf,' mumbled Jo, to no one in particular.

# 6

Lindsay packed her bag as the students left the lecture hall. All around her was the chatter of 50 people eager to start the weekend. Fridays were a drag at the best of times but sitting through a dry lecture on psychology had made them yearn for the freedom the next two days off would give them. But Lindsay didn't feel much like joining in.

She slung the heavy bag over her shoulder and climbed the stairs to the exit. The large, steeply banked lecture theatre made her feel dizzy and her legs were weary from depression rather than tiredness. She was beginning to think she'd enrolled in the wrong course and it was getting her down. Criminology had fascinated her throughout her teenage years, and she was an avid watcher of CSI type detective and forensic tv shows. Expecting to be taught detection skills, as she wanted to join the police force upon graduation, instead she had been bombarded with psychology strands. She knew that was an important part of the degree, but still… And on top of all that she was in her final year and had to decide what the subject of her dissertation would be.

As she passed through the foyer, there were free copies of the Chichester Argus, the local newspaper, on display and she grabbed one. Maybe she could find something different to do this weekend, instead of the usual drink, drink and then drink some more. Even that aspect of university life was losing its appeal.

Once at home, she dumped her stuff in her room and went into the kitchen, wrinkling her nose at the mess and smell. She threw open the windows and clicked the kettle on. Now the state of the house was starting to get her down as well. Perhaps herbal tea would help, she decided. She took the mug of boiling water back to her room and popped in a bag of green tea from the stash in her cupboard.

She lifted the local newspaper from her desk and put down the mug. As she turned the paper over to read what was on the front page, under the fold she found an article about a young woman found dead on the bank of the harbour at Bosham. There was scant information in the article, but it piqued Lindsay's interest. There weren't often murders in Chichester, a sleepy county town in West Sussex on the edge of the South Downs. The body hadn't yet been identified it said, although it was hoped that a positive identification would be made in the next few days. The article had been written by the paper's Crime Reporter, Archie Horne.

Lindsay went to her computer and pulled up the Argus' website and checked out Archie Horne. His picture suggested he was a few years older than her and his bio said he had joined the paper upon finishing his degree in journalism. He had curly black hair, a square jaw and was of Italian or Spanish heritage, if his olive skin was anything to go by. She tied her long dark hair back and reached for her mobile. Perhaps there was something to do in this godforsaken town.

Lindsay waited in the Costa Coffee for Archie the next morning. Unable to settle she checked her phone and started to chew her nails. Mentally slapping her hands down she checked her bag one more time. She had her pad, pen and copy of the paper. Her phone was fully charged so she could record any conversations. The trouble was she hadn't been entirely honest with Archie when she'd phoned him. She'd led him to believe she could help with his reporting of the murder. Which was true because of her degree, but he'd drawn inference from their conversation that she had information on the crime. Well, that was his fault, not hers. Although she could have put him straight during their phone conversation and failed to.

She sat straight backed at a small table for two and kept up her observation of the front door. She knew what he looked like from the paper's website and she told him she had long, dark hair with a wide hair band holding it back from her face.

A man walked in the door and scanned the crowd. As he caught sight of her by the window, she raised a hand and he smiled and made his way to her.

'Lindsay?'

'Yes, hi, Archie.'

'Can I get you a drink?'

'No, no I'm good thanks.'

'Okay, well, I'll, um, just...'

'Yes,' she replied, and he left to get himself a drink, bumping into several customers on the way. She wondered if he was always this bumbling. Didn't reporters have to be incisive, determined, forceful? Oh well, maybe that was why he was at a local paper and not a national.

'Hi,' Archie re-appeared and cut through her train of thought. Sitting down he said, 'Right, what do you know about this murder?'

'Ah well,' Lindsay had the grace to blush, 'I might have given you the wrong impression.'

His eyes hardened.

'What I mean is I might not have any new information, but I can help with everything else.'

'Everything else? I don't need a junior, thanks,' and he went to get up and leave.

'I'm not a bloody junior,' and Lindsay's eyes blazed to match his own. 'I'm a criminal psychologist.'

Archie had the grace to go red and sit down again.

# 7

Charlie Flood left the house to do her shift at the Student Union bar. She wasn't looking forward to it as much as she usually did. She hadn't wanted to leave her girlfriend and it was cold and damp outside, the clouds threatening more rain. She was dressed rather too skimpily for that kind of inclement weather, but it got very hot behind the bar what with all the cooling equipment and a few hundred bodies, that summer clothes were the order of the day, even in the middle of winter.

The bar was crowded as usual. If anyone knew how to party, it was students. The noise was particularly bad as there was a local band playing. Heavy metal wasn't Charlie's bag and the noise made it hard to hear the orders. Those who waggled empty bottles at her, got served more quickly than people needing to shout in her ear about gin or vodka.

Her boss pulled her to one side about 30 minutes before they were due to close. 'Alright, Charlie?'

'Yeah,' she nodded grabbing a bottle of water from under the bar and chugging down half of it.

'You seem a bit, I don't know, off tonight.'

'No, I'm okay, just tired. Got an exam tomorrow and it's on my mind, you know?'

'Don't I just. Look, I'm sure you'll be fine. Let's face it you normally are. One of the brainiest around I reckon.'

'Ah, thanks for that, Stefan.'

'No worries. Look I'm just going to change my tee-shirt. Some idiot bumped into me and drenched me in cider.'

Charlie laughed. 'I wondered what that smell was. I hadn't taken you for a big drinker.'

'No I'm not and definitely not at work. Be back in five.'

She nodded.

'Oy, Charlie!' someone shouted, and she turned and went back to serve the thirsty customer.

There wasn't much time left before she could go home to Helen. But to do that she'd have to walk through a dark alleyway, a shortcut. To be honest it had always struck Charlie as a good place to be jumped, even in daylight, never mind the dark. But it would get her home quicker and that's all Charlie cared about tonight. Maybe she'd knock this job on the head. Try and manage without the money. She'd talk to Helen when she got home. They'd make that decision together.

# 8

*Anubis, the God of Death, looked around his isolated lair and was satisfied with what he saw. He had spent many centuries as the keeper of the souls for his Pharaoh masters. Even though they were long gone, his work would continue. His mission now was ridding the world of the unclean. Those not worthy of a place in heaven. Those who were destined to live in the underworld for all eternity.*

*He had his instruments of torture.*

*He had his scales and the all-important feather.*

*He had his victim.*

*'Do we really have to do this?'*

*The voice made him pause. He hated that voice. The voice of reason. 'Yes,' he snapped, 'we do.'*

*'But this girl hasn't done anything.'*

*'Hasn't done anything! How can you say that? She is a tart and a slut.'*

*'Really? What evidence do you have?'*

*'Evidence? Evidence? How dare you!' By now Anubis was roaring. 'Did you not see the clothes she was wearing? Did you not see that place of debauchery she works in?'*

The girl who was tied to the table, joined in the conversation. Calling for help. Asking him not to hurt her. Saying she'd do anything if only he wouldn't kill her. Between her and his other self, they were beginning to get on Anubis' nerves, so he lifted his cattle prod and gave her a blast. That stunned her and reduced her to small whimpers.

To be accurate he didn't use a cattle prod on her, but a picana. An electric prod, originally based on the cattle prod, but designed specifically for human torture. It worked at very high voltage and low current to maximize pain and minimize the physical marks left on the victim. It allowed him to localise the electric shocks to the most sensitive places on her body, where they caused intense pain that could be repeated many times.

It was one of his most favoured possessions.

'Must you use that awful thing?'

'Look, butt out, will you? Leave me alone. Can't you see I'm busy preparing the instruments that I'll need for the procedure?'

They were clean and sterilised and ready for him to wield his power as Guardian of the Scales. A power that made him invincible. No one could escape him and his particular brand of justice. His latest persona was one of the better ones that he had taken the mantle of over the years. A simple soul that no one would ever suspect was really someone other. Something other. The body had served him well so far and he hoped it would continue to do so for many more years to come. But only if he'd shut up. The objective of a physical body was to enable Anubis to remain on earth. He didn't need lectures from some jumped up wimp.

As he worked, he recalled the Jumilhac papyrus that recounts a tale where Anubis protected the body of Osiris from Set. Set attempted to attack the body of

*Osiris by transforming himself into a leopard. Anubis stopped and subdued Set and then he had branded Set's skin with a hot iron rod. Afterwards Anubis flayed Set and wore his skin as a warning against evildoers who would desecrate the tombs of the dead. Priests who attended to the dead wore leopard skin in order to commemorate Anubis' victory over Set. The legend of Anubis branding the hide of Set in leopard form was used to explain how the leopard got its spots.*

*Eventually he was ready. It was time.*

*While the girl was still alive, he made the first cut from the bottom of her ribs to her belly button. He then made the further two incisions to make a 'Y'. The girl lost consciousness once he started cutting through the fat and muscle on her chest to expose her ribs. It wasn't surprising. She hadn't been given anything to dull the pain. He folded open the skin and held it in place with clamps. Underneath the ribs he could see her heart, beating erratically, but still beating.*

*He grinned. That was precisely what he had hoped for.*

*As he watched, the beating became slower, jerky, faltering.*

*He took the cutters necessary to open the ribs to give him access to the heart. That was the moment she died. Her heart couldn't take any more shocks. With practiced movements he broke through the ribs, exposing her heart. He cut it out and for a moment held it in his hand, still warm, blood flowing over his finger. He wondered how such a small organ could be capable of keeping a body alive. Without a beating heart, a person was nothing. No one.*

*He placed the heart in a container on the nearby table and took a moment to clean himself up, before moving onto the next stage.*

*'BIG, BAD WOLF.'*

*Anubis stopped. Big, bad wolf? Where had that come from? 'Was that you?' he snapped.*

*'Nope, not me. I wouldn't dare.'*

*'Good, glad to hear it.'*

*Anubis looked around the chamber. He was alone with the dead body of the girl. There was no one else there.*

*He shrugged and carried on with his work.*

'We've got an ID, Guv,' called Judith. 'Bill's just sent through the report.'

Jo and Eddie came out of her office, where they had been researching Anubis, the idea being that the more they knew about the Egyptian God, the better to understand their killer. However, Jo wasn't sure it was helping at all. All it was serving to do was to creep the two of them out.

'There she is.' Judith pulled up a picture of a young woman with black hair cut in a Vidal Sassoon sharp bob. 'Alison Rudd.'

'Her hair,' said Byrd, 'it's just like in the Egyptian pictures.'

'Maybe that's what attracts him, the sharply cut black hair,' agreed Judith.

'How come Bill found her?'

'Fingerprints,' said Judith, skim reading the report. 'It seems she was arrested when she was a teenager. Nothing major: possession of marijuana, drunk and disorderly. Looks like she was a bit of a rebel at one stage. She is also the subject of a missing persons alert.'

'What did she do for work?'

'Worked in the accounts department of a local high school.'

'Not so glamorous, nor rebellious,' said Byrd.

'Seems she saw the error of her earlier ways.'

'So in that case, where did she meet our killer?'

'That's the million-dollar question, Byrd. Come on, let's try and find out. Judith, are there any details on her living arrangements in the missing person's file?'

'Yeah, there's a flat mate called Daniel Tate.'

'Great, let's hope he'll be there to let us in. Text me the address. Oh, and get contact details for her parents from the mis per file. If they're in the area we'll see them while we're out, if not arrange for the local police to inform them, will you?'

'Boss,' agreed Judith and turned back to her computer.

It was only a short drive to Alison's flat. Jo said little on the way there, lost in her thoughts of Egyptian hieroglyphics and sharply cut black hair. Her hand strayed to her own hair. As usual put up with a large clip. As usual a bloody mess. But let's face it who had the time to diligently blow dry their hair and the money to look after it with lots of expensive products. Alison Rudd, obviously.

They pulled up opposite a purpose-built block of flats on the edge of Chichester. They both got out and Jo wrapped her tweed wool coat around her as a gust of cold wind hit them head on. 'What number, Byrd?'

'202 – so I'm guessing second floor.'

They ran across the road during a brief break in the traffic. The door to the lobby opened under Jo's hand and she raised her eyebrows at Byrd. So much for a secure entrance.

'Steps or lift?' Byrd asked.

Jo looked at him.

'Steps it is then.'

'Really, Byrd, I thought you'd know better than to ask,' she said as they reached the first floor. 'You know I hate lifts. And anyway steps are better if you're interested in burning calories.'

Mind you, Jo wasn't so much, as she was slender. The pressures of being a DI were better than any slimming plan.

They arrived at the door of 202 and could hear noises coming from within.

'Sounds like the TV,' said Byrd. 'Looks like we're in luck.'

His knock was answered by a young man with tousled hair, wearing jeans and a green rugby shirt with a white collar. Jo wasn't sure if the hair was some sort of trendy style, or if he hadn't bothered to brush it that morning. Jo and Byrd held up their identification and he seemed taken aback to find two police officers on the doorstep.

Jo introduced herself and Byrd and then said, 'And your name is?'

'Daniel Tate. I live here.'

Ah, he's on the defensive already, Jo thought.

'Do you know Alison Rudd?'

'Yes, she's my flat mate. Why?'

'I think it's best we come in, sir.' Byrd pushed the door open wider and didn't give Daniel a chance to object.

Tate stepped back, and as Jo walked into the flat, her hand brushed against Tate's bare forearm.

*She saw red. Literally. The colour filled her head.*

Her steps faltered and she almost toppled over, having to grab the back of the sofa to keep upright. But then the fleeting feeling passed as quickly as it arrived. Jo was left wondering what the red indicated. Blood? Anger? Rage? Whatever it signified, she was left with an overwhelming feeling of menace.

They were in a living room, in the centre of the flat, with doors off on either side, all of which were closed. Picture windows opposite where they stood gave a good view of the city scape.

'Can you confirm this is a picture of Alison Rudd?' Jo asked and held out her mobile to him.

Tate squinted at it. 'Yes, yes, that's her. Why?'

Jo ignored his question. 'So you share a flat with her?'

'Yes.'

'Together, as in partners?'

'No, nothing like that. I just happened to apply when Alison had an empty room and she chose me. Maybe she wanted a man around to fix stuff, or for security, you know?' Daniel put his hands in the pockets of his jeans, almost as if he were deliberately trying to look nonchalant. 'Look, what's this all about?'

Jo answered his question with another of her own. 'Is that you then? Know DIY, do you?'

'Not so much, no.'

'How about self-defence?'

'Sorry?'

'Well if Alison wanted you for security, wouldn't she have been interested in someone who had some sort of martial arts training?'

'Well, I don't know about that,' he shrugged.

'What do you know about then?'

'Well I could pay three months' rent in advance. I reckon she needed the money.'

Daniel Tate sat down but didn't offer Jo a seat. She took one anyway, leaving Byrd roaming the room. Tate ran his hands through his hair, making it look even worse than it already was, if that were possible.

'When did you last see her?'

'Must be a month ago. I'd just given her my rent. She put it in her bag and said she'd pay it into her bank while she was out.'

'Do you know if she did?'

'Did what?'

'Pay it into her bank?' Jo wasn't sure if Tate was being particularly obstructive or was just dense.

'No idea. I never saw her again.'

Jo nodded. They could check with her bank statements. If she hadn't paid it in maybe she'd been mugged for her money. But no, that wouldn't fit. She didn't think the God of Death would be much interested in a few hundred quid.

'When did you start to worry about her?'

Daniel leaned forward, his elbows on his knees. 'Dunno, after a couple of days I suppose.'

'What did you do about it? Ring the police?'

'No, I rang her parents, in case she'd gone to see them and forgot to tell me. We lived separate lives, you know, she didn't need to tell me what she was up to in detail.'

'So her parents contacted the police?'

'Yeah, someone came out to the flat and took a statement from me, but I don't think he was very interested. Kept saying that 9 times out of 10 missing adult persons return home. Just needed a few days out of their life, maybe. He told me not to worry and then left.'

Jo couldn't fault the officer who'd said that. It was standard procedure with missing adults. Unless it could be proven it was completely out of character, or they'd last been seen with someone that the police wanted to identify and question.

It was Daniel she was cross with. For not caring enough for the person he shared a flat with. He seemed to be viewing the whole thing with studied indifference. And Jo didn't like that. Not at all.

Whereas the overriding impression Jo got from the Professor was one of arrogance, with Tate it was a feeling of danger.

# 9

'Look, why are you here. What's going on?' Daniel Tate gave Jo a laconic stare.

If he was trying to intimidate her, it was never going to work. 'We've found Alison.'

'Oh,' Daniel tipped his head. 'Is she OK?'

'Not so you'd notice, no. She's dead.'

Daniel nodded. His only reaction. Was that because he already knew she was dead? Because he'd killed her? Jo had no idea. She was finding it hard to read the young man.

'We need to look in her room.'

Again he nodded.

'Where is it?' This bloke was seriously getting on her tits.

He indicated the room opposite where he was sat.

'Thank you, sir,' Jo said, laden with all the sarcasm she could muster.

Jo and Byrd went into Alison's bedroom. Byrd closed the door behind them. Jo sat on the bed and tried to get a sense of the girl as Byrd started going through drawers. A clothes tree stood in the corner with various bits of clothing on it, including several multi-coloured scarves. Handbags were lined up on the floor against one wall and her shoes displayed neatly at the bottom of the wardrobe. All the items of clothing in the room screamed "safe". Alison clearly wasn't a rebel anymore. There was nothing provocative to wear, but no sense of a style of her own either. A dressing table was topped by a mirror with photographs slotted into the frame. A couple with girl friends on a night out, but mostly of Alison alone. So she didn't seem to have a boyfriend.

Jo heard Byrd rustle papers and looked over to where he was examining the contents of a chest of drawers.

'Got her personal papers here, Guv.'

'Great, bring them all and we'll take them back to the station. Let's see what's under the bed.'

Jo got down onto her knees and lifted the duvet cover. There were several piles of books, which Jo slid out. Sifting through them she saw mostly fiction; chick lit and romance, with one or two non-fiction books. Those were mostly cookery, with two on the Egyptians. Jo did a double take.

Clambering to her feet she said to Byrd, 'Here, look what I've found,' and she brandished the books.

'Egyptians, eh? Wonder why she's got them?'

'Dunno, let's try and find out.'

Jo walked back into the living room and asked Daniel about the books.

'They're definitely Alison's. I think she had a passing interest in Egypt once. But I've never taken much notice of it, nor has she talked about it.'

Jo hadn't expected much information from him about them and it turned out she was right.

'You sure?'

'Course I am.'

Jo put the books on Egyptology on the coffee table

as Byrd came out of the bedroom carrying a couple of box files. 'Found some more personal papers on top of the wardrobe,' he grunted, struggling under the weight of them.

Jo turned to Daniel. 'That's all for now. We're taking Alison's personal papers with us. They'll be returned when we've finished with them. Thank you for your co-operation, sir.' Jo couldn't resist another sarcastic dig. She really didn't like Daniel Tate at all.

Once out of the flat, Jo said, 'Make sure we do a full background check on him. I don't trust him, nor do I believe him. Let's see what that turns up.'

'If anything, Boss.'

'Alright, if anything, but do it anyway.'

'Yes, Boss. Um, any chance of a bit of help here?' Byrd asked.

But Jo was already clattering down the stairs and didn't hear him.


Jo didn't get a chance to think about Daniel Tate for the rest of that day, as Alison's parents had been located. They lived in Dorset, having moved there on their early retirement from teaching. Maybe that explained Alison's work in a high school, she would have been used to that environment from her own education and her parent's jobs.

Jo met them at the mortuary in St Richard's, Chichester's district general hospital. She couldn't begin to understand what they were going through and that was the first thing she said to them, as well as offering her condolences. They looked decent, upright people, smartly dressed despite the occasion. She guessed they were of the generation that had to keep up standards, no matter the circumstances. They were well spoken, with Mrs Rudd's voice surprisingly quiet for a teacher. Mr Rudd was more verbose, with a clipped middle-England accent. They were certainly not of the background where you regularly found members of your family turning up dead. Jo couldn't get over the fact that Mr Rudd was wearing a tie. He must always wear one, come hell or high water. Jo thought that finding out your daughter had been killed was definitely the kind of day where you would forget to put one on. But each to their own.

'Alison was such a lovely girl,' her mother said, dabbing her eyes. 'She was kind, generous and honest to a fault.'

'She was brought up the right way,' Mr Rudd said.

'I'm sure she was,' murmured Jo.

She always found the mortuary made her whisper. She didn't want to wake the dead. Nor did she want their pleas in her head, for that would be to open a pandora's box, containing a cacophony of voices, that she'd have trouble shutting the lid on.

''Mrs Rudd, would you like to sit here, while your husband does the identification?'

'Oh no,' Mrs Rudd said indignantly. 'I need to see my daughter as well.'

'Are you sure you both want to do this?' Jo was rather alarmed by that. She would have preferred just Mr Rudd do the identification.

'Oh yes,' Mrs Rudd said quickly, before her husband could speak. 'I shan't believe it until I see her.'

'Very well. You'll see Alison on the other side of this window. Someone will come and take the cloth off her face, then replace it once you've identified her as your daughter.'

'Or not?' said Mrs Rudd and Jo could hear the hope in her voice.

'Or not. Of course,' Jo nodded. 'Ready?'

Mr and Mrs Rudd both nodded and Jo pressed a

button hidden behind the curtain on the window into the viewing room. The curtains slid open with barely a swish and there was the body on a trolley with a mortuary assistant stood next to it. The cloth was then folded over and removed from Alison's face.

Mr and Mrs Rudd gasped at the sight of their daughter, all chalk-white face and bloodless lips.

It was Mr Rudd who spoke. 'Yes, that's our daughter Alison.'

'Thank you,' said Jo.

The curtains closed and that was what broke Mrs Rudd. She collapsed onto the floor sobbing. Her husband took her in his arms, lifted her up and placed her on a chair.

'She'll be alright,' he said to Jo. 'She just needs some time.'

'Of course. Where are you staying?

'Your office have booked us a room at the Premier Inn.'

'Do you need a lift?'

'No, we have a car.'

'Very well,' Jo slid Mr Rudd a card. 'I'll be in touch tomorrow.'

'Thank you. And now if you don't mind?'

Jo could take a hint as well as the next man and she slipped away, leaving Mr and Mrs Rudd to their grief.

*Walking down the hospital corridors away from the Mortuary and towards the exit, images and sounds followed her. It started out as one or two. But as she passed wards and then the Accident and Emergency rooms, she collected more and more dead souls who, for one reason or another, had been unable to move on.*

*There were screams. Sighs. Agony. Women pleading for help as they died. Men sobbing.*

*'Tell my husband I still love him.'*

'Can you help find my daughter? My son? My wife?'

'Where am I? Why can no one hear me?'

'Help. Help. Help.'

Each one a pitiful plea that tore at her heart. Each one landing like lashes, flaying her skin.

She couldn't help them. But she couldn't outrun them either, although she tried. She hurried along the corridors, tears running down her face. It was only when she burst out of the doors at the main entrance and into the fresh air that the entreaties stopped.

Apart from one voice. That followed her for the rest of the day.

'Big, bad wolf.'

# 10

Lindsay and Archie had agreed to go to the press conference on Monday morning, together. Lindsay didn't have any lectures. Her timetable was pretty empty to give her time to research and write her dissertation. Lindsay was already waiting for Archie outside the police station when he turned up. They queued up with the other hacks and going through security Archie said that Lindsay was with him and the Argus.

Never having been to a police press conference before, Lindsay was wide-eyed. A large table was set up with four chairs behind it and microphones on it. They had been given a press pack on arrival, but it didn't say very much. Just gave the location of the body and confirmation that it was a young woman with jet black hair cut into a severe bob. A sketch of her face was included. Lindsay was grateful it wasn't a photograph of her dead.

She had been named as Alison Rudd, an employee at a local school.

'Recognise her?' Archie asked.

'No. You?'

'Nah, never seen her before. Name doesn't ring a bell either.'

Three police officers arrived, and the room settled, the noise fading as they all sat.

'Good morning,' the older man said. 'Thank you for coming. I'm DCI Crooks and with me are DI Wolfe and DS Byrd. In your press packs you have most of the information we hold on the victim. We would appreciate your co-operation in getting her description out there and ask that any members of the public who have any information to get in touch with us. We want to speak to anyone who knew Alison or saw her recently.'

Lindsay looked appreciatively at DS Byrd and figured that if all policemen were as attractive as he was, then she couldn't wait to join the force. A bit like drooling over fire fighters and the thought made her smile. Remembering where she was, she adjusted her features into a grave expression.

'Archie Horne, Chichester Argus.'

Lindsay realised Archie was speaking and tuned back in.

'How was the body found?' Archie asked.

'By a dog walker early in the morning.'

'And what was the state of the body?'

'Wrapped in bandages.' The speaker was the woman police officer, DI Wolfe.

'I beg your pardon,' Archie stammered.

'Wrapped in bandages,' Wolfe repeated.

'As in a mummy?' Lindsay said and then blushed as she realised she'd spoken out loud.

'Yes, as in a mummy.'

The room erupted and Lindsay felt the thrill that comes from investigation, no matter if you were a policeman, a journalist, or a criminal psychologist. Maybe she had chosen the right career after all.

# 11

As they filed out of the press conference, Archie took a phone call. All Lindsay heard was a mumbled conversation, as he'd turned his back on her. Once free, he confided to Lindsay that the Argus was determined to be THE local paper for coverage of the murder and that Archie was tasked by his editor with finding out about the practice of mummification. He wanted to know from Lindsay what would cause someone to want to kill a young girl and then wrap her in bandages.

'Um, well…'

'Um, well, what, Lindsay? Can you help or not?'

'There's no need to be like that, Archie. Yes, I can help but I need to go home, write some ideas up and then email them to you. Deal?'

'Yes, deal,' said Archie. 'But don't take too long, deadlines are looming.'

'Deadlines?' Lindsay was beginning to wonder what she'd got herself into.

'Yes, Lindsay, deadlines. We need to get the copy filed by 3pm this afternoon for the evening edition.'

'Crikey, right.'

'So I need your insight by 2pm. Okay? It doesn't need to be an essay, just a few helpful insights that I can weave into the story. See you later.'

Archie walked away leaving Lindsay quite stunned. But that wasn't achieving anything, so she turned and ran for home. This was her chance to put all her hard work into practice. She better man-up and get on with the job.

She didn't have far to go to get to her house. Shedding her coat and pulling her pen and pad from her bag, she wanted to read the notes she'd managed to get down. She had meant to record it on her phone but had forgotten as she had quickly become fascinated by the event.

Lindsay opened her laptop and then grabbed a couple of books off her shelf. Her initial thought was paranoid schizophrenia with delusions and possibly hallucinations. She opened the International Classification of Diseases produced by the World Health Organisation which is the reference that is used by NHS doctors.

So if their killer was schizophrenic then the first question she needed to answer for Archie was what caused it? Nobody knew exactly what caused schizophrenia as it was possibly the result of several factors. Brain chemistry, genetics and birth complications could cause schizophrenia. Some people could develop the illness as a result of a stressful event, such as the death of a loved one or the loss of a job. Stressful life events and moving to a new town or country could also trigger symptoms of psychosis and schizophrenia. There was also a solid link between the use of strong cannabis and the development of schizophrenia.

Looking at the mummification angle, their killer could have delusions. Fixed beliefs which did not match up to the way other people saw the world. Mummification was strongly linked to a practice in ancient Egypt and Lindsay therefore thought the delusion of the killer could be that he was a character from that era.

All of that, of course, was speculation, but that was the information Archie wanted. What they did with it was up to the Argus. She pressed send before she could change her mind.

Lindsay went and grabbed a copy of the paper later that afternoon and found out what Archie had done with her diagnosis. Splashed all over the front page was the story about the mummified body. He'd also used her diagnosis and decided to name their killer. Anubis: an Egyptian figure known as the God of Death.

# 12

*Once he'd cleaned himself up it was time for Anubis to perform the ritual of weighing the heart of a deceased person against Ma'at, the ancient Egyptian goddess of truth, justice, harmony and balance, who was represented by an ostrich feather.*

*The brass scales glinted in the lights Anubis had set up around the metal frame, so he had the best possible lighting as he carried out the tasks on his victim's bodies. The hanging balance scales were the nearest he could get to a replica of the ones used in Egypt all those centuries ago, with large bowls, big enough to hold a human heart. This was the way Anubis dictated the fate of souls. Hearts heavier than the feather, i.e., sinners, would be devoured. If the heart was lighter than a feather, then those souls, free of sin, would ascend to a heavenly existence with their heart intact.*

*'What do you think?'*

*'What?'*

*'What do you think? Is she a sinner or not?'*

*'Oh for goodness sake, shut up. And stop peering over my shoulder, it's getting on my nerves.'*

*As Anubis placed the ostrich feather on one side of*

*the scales he began to shake with anticipation. Would the girl's heart be free of sin? Or would he have the pleasure of devouring her heart and condemning her to the underworld for all eternity? He lifted the heart high into the air, saying a short prayer to Osiris, and then brought it down to place it on the opposite bowl.*

*It was heavier than the feather. Just as he thought. He had been right. As he always was.*

The next morning Jo decided to interview Daniel Tate again. This time at the nick. She looked at her watch, 9.30 am. 'Where does Tate work, Byrd?'

Eddie riffled through the files on his desk. Finding the right one he opened it and read, 'He's a trainer at Chichester Leisure Centre.'

'Fitness motivator.'

'Sorry, Guv?'

'That's what they're called at Westfield Leisure Centre. Fitness motivators.'

'And you know that because?'

'I made the mistake of going to the gym. Once. Never went back.'

'Not your thing?'

'Nah, I'll stick to running.' Jo was well known for her daily running habit, which suffered greatly when she was on a major investigation and didn't have the time, or the energy to run, making her grouchy. Or, some would say, grouchier than normal. 'Come on then, Byrd. Let's go. This should be fun.'

'What?'

'We're bringing him in. Going to Westfield and collecting him. What do you think?'

'You're evil,' smiled Byrd.

'I know,' Jo agreed, grinning.

Jo went for maximum effect once at Westfield. She

marched into reception, went straight to the top of the queue and brandishing her ID said, 'Detective Inspector Wolfe. Where's Daniel Tate?'

'Um…' the receptionist mumbled.

'Here, I was first,' grumbled a woman customer, but at a glare from Jo she fell silent.

'It's not a difficult question,' Jo continued talking to the receptionist. 'Where is he?'

'The, the, gym,' the spotty youth stammered.

'Thank you.'

Jo stalked across reception to the stairs, closely followed by Byrd. 'I hope you've got handcuffs on you.'

'Of course, Guv. Why? Did you forget yours?'

'I left them in my handbag in the car.'

'Really?' Then the penny dropped. 'Sorry, Guv, sarcasm.'

'You fall for it every time, Byrd,' Jo said as she climbed the stairs, grinning at him. She caught his returning grin, which made her smile even wider. She'd never noticed before, but Byrd's eyes were different colours. One was blue and one was grey. She felt drawn to them. Blinking and dismissing such thoughts she pushed through the double doors into the gym.


'Ah, there you are, Daniel,' Jo said later that morning, as she entered the interview room at Chichester police station, where they'd taken Tate.

'What do you want? I've a good mind to report you, or whatever it is, for coming to my place of work like that. Barging through the gym like a bull in a china shop and dragging me out. Oh, and telling everyone that you were the police and you wanted to question me in connection with the murder of Alison Rudd!'

'But that was simply the truth,' protested Jo.

'That doesn't mean you have to broadcast it at my place of work. I could get sacked for this,' Daniel finished miserably.

'Oh dear, never mind,' said Jo. 'Anyway, to business. Do you know where Alison was on the night she disappeared? What did she tell you? Where did she go? What was she wearing?'

'How the hell should I know? And why all these bloody questions?'

'Oh come on, Daniel, don't be dense. Because, helped by a description of what she was wearing, we can try and track her movements on CCTV throughout the city. If you can give us an idea of where she was going, we can sweep that area and perhaps see if anything can give us a clue as to what happened. So are you going to help us, or obstruct us?'

'Help, obviously. But I'm just not sure that I know anything that could help. And, of course, I'm very upset by all of this. Well, wouldn't you be? I'm a victim here too, know what I mean?'

Jo knew what he meant but didn't like it one little bit.

'At least you're still alive,' she snapped. 'Alison's lost her life. So the best thing you can do to help her, is to help us.'

'Oh very well. What do you want to know?'

'You're going to tell us everything you know about Alison.'

'Crikey, it's not much, but I'll try.'

'That's better, Daniel, thank you,' and Jo touched his hand to encourage him to talk. But all it did was send her somewhere she wasn't expecting to go…

# 13

Jo gave up around 7pm and headed for home. Perhaps a meal and a good night's sleep would help her. Maybe give her a different perspective on Tate, even. But that feeling of menace she got from him wouldn't go away.

Once at home, she put a ready meal in the oven, then took out of her oversized handbag the copies she'd taken of the paperwork. She was just pinning them up when her dad messaged.

*Free?*

*Yes come on up.*

He must have been by the door, as it opened straight afterwards, and she heard a heavy tread on the stairs. Mick was beginning to suffer from 'man in chair' syndrome and she was trying to persuade him to get out and move more. She'd even invited him to accompany her on a run, but so far he'd resisted her suggestions.

She was just pinning up a picture of Daniel Tate when Mick arrived and stood at her shoulder. He smelled of his usual Old Spice aftershave. Jo hadn't managed to persuade him to update it. He wore his usual jeans and polo shirt, which was not tucked in.

She was sure it was to hide his growing stomach and thickening waist.

'Your suspect?' he said.

'Could be. Maybe. Not sure yet,' she replied, and Jo proceeded to tell him about Daniel Tate and the reaction she'd had to him. The more she talked about Tate, the more her suspicion grew. 'The problem is, Dad, that I've not got anything that even remotely constitutes evidence.'

'Just your feeling? Your visions?'

'Yeah, that's about right.'

Mick moved along to pictures of Alison Rudd in various stages of having her bandages unwrapped at the post-mortem.

'I wanted to talk about this.' Mick pointed at Alison's mummified body at the water's edge.

'Oh yes?'

'You have a feeling about Tate, well I have a feeling about the way Alison was murdered, having her poor heart ripped from her body and then wrapped in bandages in an approximation of being mummified. Her body wasn't drained of blood was it?'

'No, nothing like that, thank God. Just wrapped in bandages. And?' Jo prompted her Dad to carry on with his thought.

'And I have a feeling she's not going to be the only one.'

'Ah, you too. Professor Russell thought the same.'

'I believe this is too ritualised to be just one killing. If he enjoyed it, he might refine his MO, but he'll do it again.'

'Are you certain of that?'

'As certain as I can be at this stage of the investigation. But I'd strongly advise that you watch out for any missing persons reports for females who look like Alison. If you get one, that could be your man again. And on that note, it smells like your supper is ready, so I'll be off.'

Jo came out of her introspection and smelled burning.

'Oh, shit,' she exclaimed and rushed to the kitchen to rescue her lasagne. When she returned to the sitting room her dad had gone.

# 14

*Anubis needed to prepare for the final stage of the ritual. He'd installed a small table-top oven specifically for this.*

*He washed and cleaned out the heart, cutting off the small stalks that had been the arteries and veins that the heart pumped blood around the body through. Past experience told him that they were hard and rubbery and indigestible.*

*Once prepared to his satisfaction, he seasoned the organ, then placed it in the pre-warmed tabletop oven he'd installed for this purpose.*

*While he was waiting for his meal to cook, he looked over his research on the next girl that needed his particular kind of justice.*

*By the time the heart was cooked, he had the beginnings of a plan in place and smiled in satisfaction as he sharpened his carving knife.*

*Once the rites and rituals were over, Anubis had one more task to perform. In accordance with Egyptian writings he had to mummify the bodies. Not having the 70 days required for the full ritual, Anubis nevertheless wrapped her in linen bandages. Some form of mummification was required, so she would be able to pass swiftly through to the underworld. Anubis believed that the mummified body was the home for this girl's soul or spirit. If her body was destroyed, the spirit might be lost. And he didn't want the soul to be lost, for it was going straight to hell, a just ending for a life of sin.*

*After one complete wrapping, he covered the bandages with warm resin and then continued with a second layer.*

*'I see you've taken my suggestion.'*

*Anubis closed his eyes and sighed. 'You again!'*

*'Well I did warn you last time. If you're putting the mummy in water, then you have to do a better job of wrapping those bandages.'*

*'I know, I heard you. Look see I'm doing it. What you said to do. Two layers with glue between them to ensure the bandages stayed in place, vital as her grave would be a watery one. There's no need to gloat.'*

*'Not gloating, just saying.'*

*'Well stop saying.'*

*'It's not as though I don't know what I'm talking about.'*

*'Shut up! Leave me be will you? Go away and bother someone else.'*

*'Sorry, I'm sure.'*

*Without the irritating voice, Anubis was able to quickly complete his task and he stood back to admire his work. All that was left was to place her in her watery grave.*


As Jo walked into the nick, the officer at the entrance said, 'Ah there you are, Guv, good timing.'

'Morning, Jed, what is it?'

'I've literally just had someone in, reporting a missing person.'

'So what has that got to do with me?' Jo tried to push away her feeling of dread. It couldn't be another, surely? But it had been two weeks since they'd found Alison and Jeremy reckoned she'd been dead two to three weeks before that.

'Look familiar?' Jed held up a photograph of a young girl.

'Jesus, she looks like my dead girl. Hang on, Jed, I'm coming round.'

Jo punched her number into the security lock on the door that kept the general public away from the police officers. She walked around to Jed's area next to the window.

'Let me have another look, would you?'

Jed handed over the photograph and Jo looked closely, seeing a young female, in her 20's, with smooth, shining black hair.

'Who is she?'

'Her name is Charlotte Flood, known as Charlie. She's local and lives with her girlfriend.'

'Her partner?'

'Yeah I think so. Anyway she's just come in, the partner. It seems Charlie has not been home for a couple of days, and no one seems to know where she is.'

'What does Charlie do?'

'She's a student at the Uni.'

'Go on,' Jo said, 'give me the file, we'll get on it. You're right, she is the spitting image of Alison. Good spot, Jed.'

'Thanks, Guv. All the contact details are in there.'

Jo walked to her office, but didn't take her coat off, dumping her bag on her chair. Walking back out she called to Byrd, 'Eddie, you're with me,' and she turned on her heel and walked towards the stairs.

Byrd scrambled to catch up with her.

'Where are we going, Boss?'

'Here.' Jo thrust the file into Byrd's hands. 'You can read it while I drive.'

# 15

Jo and Byrd were in the sitting room of a flat in another of Chichester's many blocks. They'd confirmed that they were talking to a young woman named Helen Sandford, who'd reported Charlie missing and that they were flatmates and partners.

'The thing is, Helen, why isn't Charlie on a bender somewhere?' asked Jo.

'Because she's not like that and she's missed an exam, she wouldn't do that either.' Helen twisted a handkerchief in her hands. 'This is so unlike her. I'm really worried,' she said and blotted her tears.

Jo tried to keep references to Charlie in the present tense. Maybe she wasn't their killer's victim. She was walking a fine line between being positive that Charlie would be found alive, and dread that she was the Egyptian killer's next victim. 'What is she studying?' Jo hoped it wasn't Egyptology and held her breath.

'Nursing.'

The relief was tremendous. What would studying nursing have to do with Anubis? 'How does she fund her course?'

'Loans like the rest of us and she works in a bar a

couple of nights a week.'

'Do you mind if we look at her room?' Byrd asked.

'No, of course not. We, um, we share a bedroom and made a joint study out of the second one. You might want to look at both.'

Byrd smiled at Helen. 'Thanks, we appreciate your co-operation.'

Helen tried a watery smile that didn't reach her eyes, which were becoming haunted.

Byrd and Jo looked at the bedroom but couldn't find any books on Egyptology.

'Go and check the study, Byrd,' Jo said, 'I'll check the rest of this room.'

He nodded and left, leaving Jo to sit on Charlie's side of the bed. There were medical tomes and some lighter reading. There was a silver ring, drop earrings and a rather unusual tree of life silver necklace with the addition of a gold heart hanging at the top. It looked expensive, and out of place among the costume jewellery. Jo picked it up, intending to ask Helen who had given it to Charlie.

*Immediately Jo had the sensation of falling backwards. Something was over her mouth and nose. It smelled strange, making her gag and choke. She grabbed at the arm across her chest, holding her close to her attacker. She tried to pull it away but the person holding it there was too strong. She was being dragged backwards, her shoes bumping along the floor as her legs gave way.*

*Big bad wolf.*

*And then - nothing. Only blackness. There was nothing of Charlie left.*

*Jo searched, her mind probing the darkness, but to no avail. It was as if Charlie were dead and her soul had crossed over. If that were the case, Jo hoped it was to a better, safer place.*

She jerked back into the present, still sat on Charlie's side of the bed, the chain of the necklace wrapped around her hand, biting into her flesh.

Forcing her hand to open so she could unwind the chain, she took a minute to compose herself, rubbing her hand where it had gone red with the imprint of the chain. She then walked back into the sitting room, to Helen.

'What are Charlie's interests?' Jo asked.

'I guess she likes live music and drinking. Pretty much like all of us at Uni don't you think?'

Jo nodded, remembering her own student days. 'When did you see her last?'

'Two nights ago when Charlie was leaving the flat. I was staying in to finish an assignment.'

'What are you studying?'

'History.'

'What sort of history?'

'Modern, European.'

Damn, so not Egyptology.

Byrd walked back in and said, 'Where was Charlie going when she left that night?'

'To work behind the bar at the Student Union. We kissed goodbye and she said she'd be home around 1am. But she wasn't. I woke up at 2ish and she wasn't there. I managed to fall asleep again but then woke at 5am and she still wasn't home. That's when I started to worry. After a day and then one more night alone and with no word from her, I was convinced something was dreadfully wrong and so this morning I went to the police station.'

Jo opened her hand. 'Is this Charlie's necklace?'

That brought on another bout of tears. Helen nodded. She gulped and stammered, 'Y yes. I g g gave it to her for Christmas. It was found on the floor outside the bar by one of our friends, who returned it to me yesterday. You can see the clasp is broken. It must have fallen off, when, when… Oh I don't know. I just want Charlie back!'

Jo watched, helpless, as Helen ran into the bedroom. Through the open-door Jo could see she'd thrown herself on the bed and was sobbing into a pillow.

'Byrd,' Jo called. 'I think we need coffee.'

'Boss?'

Jo indicated Helen who was still prostrate on the bed.

He nodded. 'One strong coffee coming up.'

While Byrd was opening and closing cupboards in the kitchen, Jo went into the bedroom, hugging Helen until the sobs subsided. Byrd brought in the brew and she managed to make Helen take a few gulps of coffee.

Jo stood, 'I'm sorry but we must leave. We need to get back to the station, but I will call you later. Try not to worry. Here's my card, please call me anytime, especially if you think of anything that might help us.'

Helen nodded and took the card. As they let themselves out of the flat, they could hear Helen, alone and once more sobbing for her lost love.

Once the door had closed behind them, Jo said, 'I wish we could have been able to reassure her that Charlie would be found fit and well. But I refuse to out and out lie to someone.'

'Even if it would have been a comfort and given her hope?'

'It would have been false hope, Byrd, and that wouldn't have been fair.'

They reached Jo's car and clambered in. On the way back to the station Jo said, 'We need to find out if our first girl, Alison Rudd, had a bar or pub job. There are links in there somewhere, I know there are. We just have to find them.'

'If Charlie turns out to be our next victim.'

'And Eddie, find out where Danial Tate's been over the last couple of days.'

'Really, Guv?'

'Really,' and Jo deliberately turned away to make a point of concentrating on the traffic, ensuring there would be no further discussion on the subject.

# 16

Jo hurried back to the office, hoping against hope that Charlie might have been found. But just like the hope she refused to give Helen; her own hope was swiftly extinguished. There was nothing. No sightings. But there was no body. Jo decided to be thankful for small mercies.

'We need someone to go up to the University. Let's see if Charlie did her shift at the Union.'

Jo thought she did and that she was taken afterwards but couldn't mention her vision.

'And if anyone saw her leave with someone, either willingly, or against her will. We've a photograph of her in an approximation of the clothes she was wearing when she left the flat. Short denim skirt, Union tee-shirt and blue sweatshirt with a hood. Her partner Helen can't remember what shoes she was wearing. She also had a small black rucksack with her. Judith, can you get those details out to the patrols ASAP and send this picture with the message. Byrd, I want you to see Tate. Do we know where he is right now?'

'Yeah, the surveillance team called in a while back. He's gone to work at Chichester Leisure Centre.'

'Excellent. Go and find out where he was the past couple of nights. Don't ring first. I want him on the back foot and not on the front. Understood?'

'Yes, Boss,' agreed Eddie, but not with any enthusiasm.

'Anything else I should know?' Jo looked at Judith.

'Yes. Bill has sent over another forensics report from the examination of Alison's body and bandages.'

'And?' There was that hope again.

'Nothing. She'd been dead too long and in a watery grave. According to Bill we didn't stand a cat in hell's chance of finding anything useful. And it seems he was right.'

'Bollocks.'

'Sorry, Guv.'

'Alright, let's send someone up to Alison Rudd's school, to try and find out if she had any friends there, ones that she saw outside work. Anyone who might know what her social life was like. Can you organise that, Byrd?'

Byrd gave a stiff nod. Jo could sense she'd irritated him. She just didn't like Tate and knew, because of her feelings, that he was the sort who could be capable of harming another human being. He exuded a feeling of menace. He didn't seem to have any empathy for his flatmate at all. He didn't seem to care one jot about what had happened to her. In Jo's book that wasn't on. So she didn't care what Byrd thought. She had a duty not to leave any stone unturned and she was determined to do it. For Alison's sake. Even if it meant her looking like a bloody fool at the end of it. She could live with that. The trade-off would be worth it.

# 17

Anubis walked around his lair. His latest victim had been found to be a sinner, just as he thought, and she would soon be on her way to the halls of hell.

'What's wrong with you?'

'Nothing, stop poking your nose.'

'No, come on, I'm serious. What's wrong?'

'Well if you really must know, I wish I could find someone worthy of my ritual. Someone who's heart is lighter than the feather. Someone who would be on their way to meet Osiris. I have been practicing the awakening of the dead ritual.'

'What's that when it's at home?'

'Well, once the weighing of the scales has been completed and the soul found to be pure, then it's my job to awaken the soul. In Egypt the mummy is removed from the sarcophagus when it arrives at the door of the tomb and is placed upright against the wall by a priest wearing the mask of Anubis, thought to have become me.'

'That's a bit rich. Someone imitating you.'

'It's alright, it happens all the time. Anyway for a person's soul to survive in the afterlife it will need to *have food and water. The opening of the mouth ritual was thus performed so that the person who died could eat and drink again in the afterlife and be able to see and hear as a living being.'*

*'That's pretty cool, I guess. Anyway what's all over the walls?'*

*'Those are copies of the pictures of the ceremony taken from the pyramids. I would prefer them to be etched into the walls, just as they are in the ancient tombs, but I just don't have the time for that. Anyway it's time you pushed off. I'm busy preparing for my next victim.'*

As Eddie schlepped off to do her highness' bidding, he decided to take a young detective constable with him. She needed the experience and he needed the company. Plus she was pretty good to look at.

'Sandy, you're with me,' he called as he walked out of the office, not waiting for her. He'd dispatched two officers to follow up at Alison's school.

Jill Sandy was a newbie who had joined the force, done her training at police college and then her two years in uniform on the beat. She was no push over on the streets, but at times seemed out of her depth in an office environment. She was intelligent but had yet to find her way around an investigation. It was early days and Byrd wondered if this case would be the making of her. It might be the breaking of her, of course. In fact it could mean the breaking up of the team if they couldn't crack this one. The trouble was Eddie was afraid the Boss was clutching at straws with this Daniel Tate angle. But, to be honest, they didn't have anything else to go on, or any other suspects in the frame.

Jill Sandy caught up with Eddie at the front door of the station, coat half off, hair all over the place and a handbag that was threatening to dump its contents on the floor.

Eddie said, 'Hang on, Sandy, get yourself together first,' and watched as she straightened her clothes, smoothed down her hair and zipped up her handbag.

'Right, Sarge, sorry.'

Eddie grinned at her. 'Come on, you, let's get this over with.'

Driving to the leisure centre, Byrd gave her the background to Daniel Tate. 'He's Alison Rudd's flatmate, but a particularly uncaring one. The Guv has taken an instant dislike to him and wants us to keep needling him.'

'Do you think he's our man, Sarge?'

Byrd didn't want to be disloyal, so didn't tell Sandy what he really thought, merely saying, 'The jury's still out on that one. It's our job to check his alibi and to see how he reacts to another visit by the police.'

'Yes, Sarge. Understood.'

Byrd doubted that she did understand, but at least she was making the right noises. Once at the centre, he nodded for Sandy to introduce them at Reception. It was the same spotty youth from the other day.

She flashed her ID and said, 'DC Sandy and DS Byrd, Chichester Police. We'd like to see Daniel Tate, please.'

'He's busy.'

'Oh!'

'With a client. Doing one to one personal training.'

'When will he be free?'

Byrd couldn't take anymore and was in danger of laughing at Sandy and that would never do. Stepping forward he said, 'Where is he?'

'Um, the gym.'

'Come on, Sandy,' and he turned away and made for the stairs with Jill running after him.

At the top she said, 'Sorry, Sarge, got that a bit wrong, didn't I?'

'We're the police, Sandy, on a murder enquiry. We don't have time for nice. We're not trying to foster community relations. You need to forget all you've learned so far in the force. Being a detective is the complete antithesis of being on the beat. Understand?'

'Yes, Sarge,' she puffed up the stairs.

'Oh and you need to get your fitness up. You're spending most of your time in a chair now, not walking several miles a day.'

'Maybe I should get some one to one training from Daniel Tate.'

Byrd raised an eyebrow, but as a quick come back, he had to acknowledge that it wasn't bad. There was hope for Jill Sandy yet.

Daniel Tate was getting an eye full of his client's assets when Jill and Eddie found him in a quiet corner of the gym.

Straightening up, Tate said, 'What the hell do you want now? Can't you see I'm busy?'

'Just a few moments of your time please, sir,' Eddie said, which could be taken one of two ways. As being polite, which the client would see it as, or being sarcastic, which Tate would see it as.

'Carry on with that. Five on each side.'

Tate left his client to her work out and walked through the double doors out of the gym, waiting for them at the top of the stairs.

'Is this really necessary?' he demanded of Byrd.

'Yes. We've another missing girl.'

'What's that got to do with me?'

'Can you account for your movements last Saturday and Sunday?'

'Um, no not really. What can I say? It was the weekend.'

'Where did you go?'

'Not sure. I must have been drinking as I had a hell of a hangover on Sunday morning.'

'Where? Who with?'

'Can't remember. Must have blacked out.'

'Sunday night?'

'Could have gone out again. Might have stayed in. Who knows? Sorry I can't be of more help,' and Tate left them standing there and returned to his client.

'He's a real piece of work, Sarge.'

'Don't I know it. But not liking him doesn't mean he's a killer.'

'So what do we do now?'

'Watch and learn, Sandy.'

Byrd pushed through the door, back into the gym.

Reaching Tate he said in a loud voice, 'Daniel Tate, I am DS Byrd from Chichester Police. I need you to accompany me to the station to make a statement concerning your movements last Saturday and Sunday nights in connection with the disappearance of Charlotte Flood.'

'What?' Daniel Tate looked at them with disbelief.

His client had stopped her work-out and was watching with undisguised interest.

'Are you going to come quietly, sir, or must I use force?'

By now the whole gym was watching the free show.

'No, no, I'll come quietly,' and Tate stalked out of the gym, quickly followed by Byrd and Sandy.

# 18

Tate refused to speak during the short car journey and Byrd was glad to leave him in an interview room once they arrived back at the police station.

He rang upstairs to tell Jo they were back and hung around the corridor waiting for her. 'I'm beginning to hate the idiot as much as you, Boss,' Byrd confessed to Jo when she arrived.

As they walked through the door, Tate jumped to his feet. 'Are you deliberately trying to ruin my whole life? I've done nothing! Why don't you believe me?' he shouted.

'Because you're a lying piece of shit,' growled Byrd. 'So sit down.'

'Actually Byrd, that's not quite right,' Jo said.

'Thank you, Inspector.' Tate looked suitably smug.

'He's an obnoxious, lying piece of shit, who doesn't care about anyone other than himself.'

Byrd tried hard not to laugh. 'Thank you, Inspector,' he said. 'I couldn't have put it better myself.'

'So,' said Jo turning to Tate, 'have you had any more thoughts about Alison? Recalled any facts?'

'Like what?'

'We still haven't found her clothes. What was she wearing when she left the flat for the last time?'

'I've told you I don't know.'

'A skirt?'

'No, I never saw her wear one. She always dressed in jeans.'

'Good start. Blue jeans?'

'No, she had some new black ones on.'

'Oh, now we're getting somewhere. And you know they were new because?'

'She'd shown them to me. She was all excited because she'd got some new clothes. They were only from Primark, but still.'

'Interesting. Why was she buying them?'

'Eh?'

'Did she not have many clothes? Had she got some extra money, so she thought she'd treat herself? Or maybe she had a special event that she was going to?'

'Oh I see what you mean. Um, well she seemed much happier since she started that group thing.'

'Group thing?'

'Yeah it was up at the University.'

Jo held her breath. Could this be the link? Why hadn't he told them this before?

'What group, Daniel?'

'To be honest I'm not really sure.'

'How do you know it was up at the University?'

'Because I saw her there.'

'Saw her?'

'Yeah, several times when I was teaching up at the University gym. You know, personal trainer stuff and all that.'

Once Tate had gone, Jo gathered the team around the board. With barely controlled anger, she said, 'Why didn't we know Daniel Tate worked at the University gym?'

Everyone looked very sheepish, but no one was brave enough to answer.

'Because we haven't done the usual background checks. Correct?'

'Yes, Guv.'

'Sorry, Guv.'

'Isn't that standard procedure when we identify a suspect?' Jo stood ramrod straight with clenched fists.

'Yes, Boss,' said Eddie. 'Look, we fucked up,' he looked around at the team. 'Let's put it right and do a full background check on him. It's not possible to make everyone feel worse than they do already. What do you say, Boss?'

'Very well,' she agreed, but inside was still seething, annoyed with herself as much as anyone. She should have directed someone to do the job. She'd failed just as much as her team.

'We've put the transcript of the interviews at Alison Rudd's school on your desk, Boss,' said Jill.

'Thanks,' and Jo turned on her heel and stalked back to her office.

Slamming the door behind her made her feel slightly better and she walked around her desk to read the information on Alison Rudd.

Jo's first impression was that Jill Sandy had done a good job with her summary of the interview. Skills like that would stand her in good stead in any future investigations. She made a mental note to add that compliment to Sandy's personal file.

She'd interviewed the Head Teacher and other administrative colleagues. The general consensus was that Alison had worked hard and had been well liked. Sandy had asked if Alison had had any outside hobbies or interests, but none of them knew of any and didn't think she did. It seems she had been totally focused on work, always went the extra mile and seemed to intuitively know what was needed next. She found solutions to problems and implemented them.

It appeared their dead girl had been out to make an impression in her job and perhaps didn't have much of a work/life balance. Jo reached for the phone and rang Jill Sandy.

'Jill, why do you think Alison was so work focused? Did you get a sense of the reason for that?'

'Oh, right, well, no one had a bad word to say about her. There was no gossip, no hint of slacking or scandal. The only thing I can come up with is that perhaps she was trying to atone for her previous life. We know she'd been picked up on minor drugs charges in the past. When I asked why she wasn't a teacher like her parents, colleagues said she used to tell anyone that asked, that she'd decided a teaching career wasn't for her. She'd preferred facts and figures.'

'Thanks, Jill and good work.'

Jo replaced the receiver, reflecting on the fact that Alison Rudd had worked hard at turning her life around and it seemed so unfair that after all that effort she should lose it at the hands of some maniac. Jo was still sure that Daniel Tate was firmly in the frame. But one thing still niggled her. They'd not turned up any evidence that Daniel was into Egyptology, apart from those two books hidden under Alison's bed. That was one conundrum Jo was still puzzling over.

# 19

The next morning Jo was woken by the ringing of her mobile. It would stop, then start again incessantly ringing and buzzing and generally making a nuisance of itself. Finally she answered it.

'Yes?'

'Morning, Boss,' said the cheerful voice of Eddie Byrd. 'Sorry to wake you, but we've got another one.'

'What?' Jo sat up in bed.

'A second body.'

'With bandages?'

'Yes.'

'Drive over and pick me up.'

'I'm already here.'

Jo tumbled out of bed and looked out of the window. There was Byrd and he raised a hand in greeting. She ended the call and hurried to the bathroom.

The crunching of gravel under her feet on her way to the car made her wince. Her watch showed 6 am and she didn't want to wake her father. Although that was rather a moot point as glancing up at the house, she saw him raise a hand in greeting from his first-floor bedroom. No doubt he'd be round when she eventually made it home that night to be brought up to date on the case.

Byrd drove carefully but swiftly down into Chichester, once more heading for Bosham. This time they arrived while the mummy was still in the river. The body was being held by a long pole with a hook on the end while the divers got into position to bring her out. Jo realised she was calling the mummy a 'she' in her mind but guessed that was understandable. It looked like her father was right – their killer had struck again with a similar MO.

Bandages were strewn out behind the body like trailing seaweed, bobbing around her as though they had a life of their own. It reminded Jo of the head of Medusa and hoped they wouldn't all be turned to stone for looking at it. Jo kept getting glimpses of black hair that had become loose where the bandages had begun to unravel around her head. It was the most poignant sight she had ever seen, and she once more resolved to finding the twisted bastard who was doing this.

'You alright, Guv?'

'What? Yes fine, Byrd. By the way, thanks for the lift and for the coffee.' She tipped her take away cup at him turning her thoughts away from the dead girl.

'No worries, Boss. Glad to be of service.'

Those sharp eyes of his smiled into hers and Jo found she had to look away and swallow. Hard. Behave, she admonished herself. This was certainly not the time, not the place, and probably not the right kind of attraction to feel. They worked together. She was his boss. It was totally inappropriate to have those sort of feelings for a subordinate. But on the other hand, his sense of humour, his little acts of kindness, those bloody eyes and that tight arse. What on earth was wrong with her? She was never like this.

She was saved from her thoughts by the shout, 'We've got her!'

The mummy was carefully taken out of the river by two divers and placed on the blue plastic sheeting that had been laid out on the bank. There seemed to be some sort of chain around her waist.

'What's that chain?' shouted Jo.

A third diver emerged from the river, struggling with what looked like a concrete block.

'Bloody hell,' said Byrd, who'd appeared by her side. 'It looks like she'd been weighted down.'

A diver approached them, taking off his goggles and his mouthpiece. 'She was weighted down,' he agreed. 'But your bloke is crap at judging the tides. She was exposed at low tide. He'd made the chain too long. Bloody idiot,' he finished and went off to get changed.

Just then Bill Burke turned up. 'Right, everyone suited up please,' he called. 'And where's my bloody tent? Let's not contaminate my scene more than absolutely necessary.'

Jo didn't think he'd get anything from the riverbank as per the previous body, but kudos to Bill for trying his best.

'I don't think there's much we can do here, Byrd,' she said. 'Let's wait until she's at the mortuary.'

# 20

Once back at the office, she called the Professor. 'Morning, Prof Russell, it's Jo Wolfe from – '

'Chichester Police,' he finished for her. 'What can I do for you?'

'What's the deal with this mummification?'

'I'm sorry?'

'Why did Anubis wrap the bodies up? I'm trying to get a hold of how our killer thinks.'

'Um, okay, well the name Anubis is from the Greek form of the Egyptian and means 'to decay'. That shows us that he had an early association with death. Later he had many other names and titles.'

'Which were?'

'Lord of the Sacred Land and He Who is Upon the Sacred Mountain, both refer to the area surrounding a necropolis.'

'A necropolis?' queried Jo.

'A graveyard, or burial site. The other two main ones would be, He Who is in the Place of Embalming and Foremost of the Divine Booth, both talking about Anubis being in the embalming booth and the burial chambers.'

'Chambers?'

'Yes, within the palaces or within the pyramids. The pyramids would be for the royals and their courtiers. Those of a lowly standing would be placed in tombs cut from the rocky site around the pyramid.'

'All underground then.'

'Yes. Does that help?'

'Not sure yet,' said Jo being evasive. 'One more thing. What's with the head gear?'

'The head of the jackal?'

'Yes, that's the one.'

'That's how Anubis was depicted in the pictures etched into the walls of the pyramids. We believe it came from him keeping the grave sites free of jackals. Priests representing Anubis at the preparation of the mummy and the burial rites may have worn these jackal-headed masks in order to impersonate the god. They were certainly utilized for processional use as this is depicted representationally and is mentioned in late texts. The many two- and three-dimensional representations of Anubis which have survived from funerary contexts, indicate the god's great importance in this aspect of Egyptian religion, and amulets of the god were also common.'

Jo was beginning to feel as though she were listening to a lecture up at the University. 'So to sum up,' she said. 'We're looking for an underground embalming site and for a bloke wearing a jackal head mask. Thanks, Professor.'

Jo cut the call and leant back in her chair. She was sure the Professor could have churned more and more bits of information on Anubis and the last thing she wanted was to have him going on a her for the next 30 minutes. She wasn't sure the information he'd given her would help find Anubis' lair, but would help her recognise it when she did.

# 21

Jo didn't have to wait long for the post-mortem. They were called to the mortuary within a couple of hours.

'I've got a free slot,' explained Jeremy. 'So I thought I'd push your girl to the top of the queue.'

'Thanks, we really appreciate it,' said Jo. 'The sooner we can get on this the better chance we might have of finding this sick bastard.'

'Exactly, so let's get started.'

Everything went to plan, with Jeremy carefully revealing the body and Bill collecting evidence as they went along. Jo was impressed by the easy professionalism of the two men and was glad she had them on her team.

As the girl's head was revealed, Jo immediately recognised Charlie Flood.

'Oh, dear,' she whispered.

But Byrd heard her. 'I know, I'm sorry, Boss. I think we were all hoping it wouldn't be her.'

'This will devastate Helen.'

Byrd didn't reply but nodded his agreement. He then looked more closely at Charlie. 'Hang on,' he said. 'Didn't she have long dark hair?'

'Yes, why?' asked Jo moving to get a better view of the body.

'He's cut it!'

So he had. Their killer had cut the victim's hair off at the jaw line, in an approximation of an Egyptian hair style. Tears threatened and Jo had to turn away while she battled her emotions.

She was blinking away the tears when Jeremy said, 'You need to see this, Jo.'

'What?' she turned to face him and saw that he'd opened the bandages across Charlie's chest. As per Alison's body there was a long cut along her chest, her ribs had been prised open and the heart was missing. 'Her heart's been taken out,' she said. 'Just like Alison.'

'Yes, but it's been put back into the chest cavity.'

Jo leaned in closer. 'Why has he done that?'

'Don't know, that's your job. But there's something else.'

'What?'

'Her heart's been cooked.'

Jo looked in horror as Jeremy lifted Charlie's heart from her body. She could see it was a different colour, brown instead of red and raw. There was only half of it.

'Where's the other half?'

'I reckon he's eaten it,' said Byrd.

Jo ran for the ladies' toilet, where she threw up the two cups of coffee she'd drunk that morning.

## 22

Jo and Eddie were in the car park, gulping fresh air and she was trying to stop trembling. It was as if she were shivering, but she wasn't cold as she was wrapped in her tweed coat. It was this case. She'd never known anything like it. She'd dealt with some bad things before, but this one… There was nothing she could do about the horror, she had to get hold of her emotions and finish this. Her feelings must take a back seat and she had to focus on the things she could control, instead of the ones she couldn't. What she should focus on was their investigation. That was the best way of getting justice for the victims of the sick bastard doing this. But she had to admit this was one of the times when she wished she still smoked.

Her days were filled with fear that they'd hear of another missing girl and her nights… Well, they were full of horror.

Wolves howling at the moon, then their open mouths turned her way. She was close enough to smell their rotting breath, to see the saliva drip from their jagged, sharp teeth. Fangs. They lunged at her, going for the kill, aiming for her throat.

Big bad wolf.

There were Egyptian hieroglyphics that she couldn't understand. Painted on the chamber walls, from floor to ceiling, they told the story of Anubis, God of Death. Threat hung in the air, thick enough to taste. There was no way out. She was trapped, with the walls slowly coming towards her. She backed up against one wall, only to feel it move, pushing her forward, rocks grating together, grinding and squealing.

Girls tied up on metal tables, naked, cold, terrified. She felt the jabs of a cattle prod, saw red marks appear on her skin.

And then there was the claustrophobia. Underground tunnels that she couldn't find her way out of. Dim lighting hindering her. Running and running, with nowhere to go. Coming up against brick walls and having to back track. All the time the cries of the wolves carried to her on the fetid air.

Big bad wolf.

She gulped but didn't manage to get any more air into her lungs. She felt as though she were doomed to die in Anubis' lair.


Shaking away the remembered nightmares, she said, 'Come on, Byrd. You can drive,' and she threw him the car keys.

'Where are we off to, Boss?'

'We have to see Helen Sandford and tell her that her partner is believed to be dead.'

'Shit.'

'I know, but it has to be done and I'd rather it was us that did it.'

It was only a short drive and they were there too soon. Jo gave Byrd a watery smile as he turned off the ignition.

'You alright?' he asked.

Jo nodded. 'Come on, let's do this.'

They climbed the stairs to Helen's flat and she answered at the first knock.

'Any news?' The hope in her eyes was almost the undoing of Jo.

'Can we come in, Helen?' Byrd said.

Helen nodded and backed away from the door.

Refusing a seat, Jo said, 'Helen, I'm sorry to tell you that we recovered a body from Chichester Harbour today…'

'No, no, please don't tell me it's her.'

'I'm sorry, but we have good reason to believe it's Charlie.'

'NO!' Helen crumpled like a marionette whose strings had been cut and she fell to the floor sobbing. Byrd helped her up and led her to the sofa. He took a clean handkerchief out of his pocket and handed it to her.

She looked up at the two police officers, sobbing and gulping, then managed to say, 'Do I have to identify her? I don't think I can do that. Oh what am I to do without her?' Helen wailed.

Jo was upset for Helen, but a small part of her thought that perhaps the girl was being a touch melodramatic, as Helen screamed and sobbed. But what did she know? Never having been through a death of a partner. Her mother had died when Jo was only three years old and in all honesty she didn't remember her. Then the unwelcome thought of her dad dying sent chills down her spine.

Helen continued to cry, but the storm was abating, subsiding into hitching breaths.

'Byrd, would you make Helen some tea please?'

He nodded. As he left the room Jo said, 'I'm just going to double check your bedroom and study.OK?'

Helen nodded and Jo slipped away. She found what she wanted in the bedroom. In many of the photos of the couple in the flat, Charlie was wearing a ring on the 4th finger of her left hand. It looked like the engagement ring Princess Diana wore, a large sapphire surrounded by diamonds and Jo found it in a trinket dish on the dressing table. Jo picked it up and held it in her hand, it was just costume jewellery, but she was sure it meant a great deal to Helen and Charlie. Jo took several deep calming breaths and then, with a frisson of fear, slipped it on her own finger.

*She was enveloped with a sense of the deep love between the couple, feelings of happiness and contentment. But then other emotions began to break through, as though they were lightning strikes.*

*Hate. Fear. Anger. There was pain. Darkness.*

*Jo was bombarded, pushed this way and that as the strikes hit her again and again. A woman's voice called out for help and then with a final bloodcurdling scream it was over.*

Jo was left alone, the vision fading. There was nothing else the ring could tell her.

Glancing in the bedroom mirror Jo wiped away the tears that had been streaming down her face. 'I'm so sorry,' she whispered. 'Sorry I couldn't save you.'

She replaced the ring in the dish and returned to the living room just as Byrd was handing a mug of tea to Helen. 'Ah, there you are, Boss. Everything okay?'

'Fine thanks, Byrd. Right, we'll get Charlie's parents to do the formal identification and I'll ask them to visit you afterwards, Helen. Is that alright?'

'Yes, thank you,' said Helen her hands wrapped around the mug. 'I appreciate all you're doing. I know you'll try your best to find Charlie's killer.'

Byrd and Jo could only nod and then left the flat, closing the door quietly behind them.

# 23

The second death stunned Archie and Lindsay. Archie had been dripping a little more information every day to keep the story alive in the paper, including background on the poor victim, Alison Rudd. The police wouldn't speculate if they had a suspect or not, so that was a dead end. The new victim was quickly named as Charlie Flood and her body had also been wrapped in bandages.

Archie and Lindsay met at Costa Coffee which was quickly becoming their regular haunt.

'So what do you think?'

'About?' asked Lindsay wiping milk from her latte off her lip.

'The fact that he's taken another girl and wrapped her in bandages as well.'

'It kind of reinforces my diagnosis. The fact that he's done it twice now, confirms a delusion.'

'This bloke is really nuts then?'

Lindsay threw him a look. 'Honestly, Archie, paranoid schizophrenia is a mental illness.'

'I know, but you've got to have a screw loose to be going around killing young girls.'

'Perhaps you had better focus on the girls for now.'

'Such as?'

'Are they a type? Are there any connections between the victims, or individually between the killer and the victim?'

'I know,' huffed Archie. 'I am the reporter.'

'Well get on and report,' Lindsay said and left him sitting there staring into his coffee cup as though that's where the answers were.

Lindsay was more interested in what could have triggered their killer's delusion. But she couldn't think straight in the noise of the café. She needed to go home and get her thoughts in order and collect as much information on the case as she could glean from the newspapers and from the internet.

# 24

Back at the office, Judith had found Charlie on CCTV. Byrd grabbed them coffees and then they met in Jo's office to look at the footage. Judith had already isolated the parts with Charlie in them.

'There she is, Boss,' said Judith and pointed to the screen. They watched a girl come out of the Student Union, with lights going out in the building behind her. The girl's clothing was similar to that described by Helen; short skirt with hoodie on over it.

'She's leaving after finishing her shift,' Judith explained. 'She stops for a moment and lights a cigarette.'

They watched as the campus cameras picked Charlie up as she walked in the direction of the town centre. She didn't meet anyone, nor was anyone else shown on the film. In the silent CCTV footage, it was as if she was the only one left alive in some sort of weird dystopian world.

Then she seemed to disappear into thin air.

'Where did she go?' Jo asked.

'That's the problem,' said Judith. 'There is one place that is a black spot just outside the campus grounds. It's just our luck she had to walk through that bit. Who knows where she went from there?'

'And you can't find her anywhere else after that?'

'Not at the moment, Boss, because I don't know which way she would have walked. Also there could be an alleyway or something she walks through that I don't know about.'

'Shit!' Jo thought for a moment. 'Did she meet someone? Where there any cars in the area that seemed to be patrolling, waiting for someone or looking out for someone? Judith get onto that. Byrd get in touch with Helen and get the exact route Charlie would have taken from the campus to their home. Then Judith can follow that up as well. Come on guys, there must be something. There has to be. Oh, and get Tate back in, Byrd!'

Jo stormed out of her office leaving Byrd and Judith watching her depart with open mouths.

She banged through the door of the ladies and shrugged off the worry about what the team would think of her. It was more important that she stop her hands from shaking. She scooped up cold water onto her face in an effort to cool the heat of her emotions.

Deciding that showing how she was feeling wouldn't do any harm, Jo slumped against the wall. In fact if the team saw her getting emotional about a case, it could spur them on to do better, faster work.

And that had to be good. Didn't it?

# 25

Jo caught Jill Sandy sitting at her desk, out of the corner of her eye. So she headed over there.

'Jill, how's the background checks coming along on Daniel Tate?'

'Oh, hi, Boss. Hang on,' Jill went through the files on her desk and Jo was left waiting, tapping her foot in annoyance.

'Here's a copy of my report for you, Boss,' Jill said and passed Jo a buff file. 'I've interviewed Tate's colleagues, present employer and asked around the centre what people think of him.'

'And?'

'Oh, he seems to do a good job, but he's not universally well liked. A number of them thought he was a bit weird.'

'Weird?'

'Yes, he comes across as a bit of a loner, quiet, introvert, which is strange for someone who works in a leisure centre and has to deal with the public daily. The rest of the employees are upbeat, chatty and complimentary to their clients. Daniel is the complete antithesis.'

'Unfortunately being a loner doesn't automatically make him a killer.'

'Exactly, Boss.'

'Does he have a life outside of work?'

'Not much that I can find out about. People said he seems to stay in a lot and has never joined in on nights out with the rest of the team.'

'He's a bit of a queer fish, isn't he?' Jo mused.

'Rather odd, but not necessarily bad.'

'Mmm,' Jo flicked through the papers. 'Is he still at the flat?'

'Yes. I rang and asked him about that, saying that we needed to know if he was moving on and what his new address was going to be.'

'How come he's still in the flat then?'

'Alison's parents had been paying the mortgage because they hoped she would come back. Now they know she's dead, they intend to put it up for sale. They've given him a month to find a new home. He said that it sucked.'

'It's better than being dead,' said Jo and walked away.

# 26

Later that night was the first chance she'd had to talk to her dad over the last few days. He came up the stairs at Jo's insistence, dressed in pyjamas with a sweatshirt pulled over the top. Jo had to laugh at the state of him as he grumbled about just having climbed into bed and then having to get out again. Did she not realise that he was an old man these days who needed his sleep? Which made Jo laugh all the louder.

'Right, now we've got that out of the way,' said Mick. 'How's things with the case?'

'Pretty bloody awful, Dad, if the truth be known. I've got a first suspect that I can't pin down, and a Professor who rates himself as the font of all knowledge on Anubis, but who isn't helping in the slightest.'

'What about the dead girls? Anything from them?'

'I got hold of a ring from our latest girl, Charlie.'

'And put it on?'

Jo nodded.

'Bad?'

Again she nodded. 'It was more feelings than anything else. Hate, anger, fear,' Jo shuddered as she

92

remembered the onslaught. 'But it was the all-pervading sense of sadness. And then the scream at the end.'

'As she died?'

'I reckon so.'

Jo sat down, hands shaking, tears threatening.

Mick went into the kitchen and after a short while came back with two glasses of red wine. 'Here,' he said handing her one. 'I think we both need this.'

Jo nodded and took a couple of mouthfuls, glad for the warming effect of the alcohol and it's calming influence.

Ever since Jo's riding accident, when she was thrown from a horse that bolted during a ride out on the South Downs and which resulted in a fractured skull and a six-month coma, she'd had what her father termed as her gift. If she touched someone who had died, or handled a possession that meant something to them, she received vibrations or visions, relating to their death. It had started with a visit to her elderly aunt who had died and was in a viewing room in the undertaker's premises. She'd held her aunt's hand, immediately experiencing severe pains in her chest, breathlessness and feeling of panic. Unbeknown to Jo, her aunt had died of a heart attack and Jo had relived it. Realising this might be as a direct result of the accident, she never mentioned it to anyone at the time. Later that night, alone with her father, she'd confessed to touching her aunt and told him everything.

Together they'd gone to the local spiritualist church and talked to some of the members. At the time Jo was very sceptical, but as the evidence mounted that she did indeed possess an ability to read the dead or occasionally a possession of theirs, she'd tried to use it for good in her job. She found the more she did this the stronger the feelings or visions were. It was a bit like learning a new skill, it got better with practice. It was harder to read another living person. Sometimes she got feelings from a touch or a handshake, but they were never as vivid or reliable as when she was touching the dead.

But she never talked about it to anyone other than her dad. Ever.

'It's all very well having this gift, as you call it,' said Jo. 'But how does it help? We know how the girls died, but not why and not where. I'm not getting that from the dead.'

'Aren't you?'

'I don't think so.'

'What about the first girl? Alison?'

'What about her?' Jo wasn't sure where he was going.

'When you touched her didn't you get a sense of where she was?'

Jo thought back. Then said, 'She appeared to be in an underground chamber. Brick walls, dirt floor, no windows. The overall impression was of a crumbling, abandoned space.'

'Exactly.'

'Dad do you know where I would find such a place?'

'Well no. But you can start looking.'

'Where?'

'There must be some. For God's sake stop being defeatist.'

'Defeatist!' Jo shouted. 'How bloody dare you!' she jumped to her feet. 'I'll get someone on it first thing tomorrow!'

Mick laughed. 'There you go, that's my girl!'

'You bugger,' she said. 'For that you can get me another glass of wine.'

## 27

'Byrd, come in, would you?' Jo saw Eddie passing her office door and called him in.

'Guv?'

'I've got Professor Russell on the line. I thought it would be good to have someone else listening in.'

'Okay,' said Byrd. 'Let's do it,' and he sat opposite Jo on the other side of her desk.

Jo picked up her phone and pressing the 'speaker' button said, 'Morning, Professor Russell.'

'Morning, Detective Inspector.'

'What can I do for you?' Jo had no idea why he was calling her.

'I just wanted to give you an alternative view of the God Anubis.'

'Really?'

'He wasn't all bad, you know.'

'No, I don't know. Enlighten me.'

Jo couldn't see any way that their killer could justify what he was doing. But hey, she had to admit she knew nothing about Egypt and its Gods. And if their killer was using Anubis as a role model, she guessed she needed to hear what the Prof had to say.

'Well, we know that Anubis was central to every aspect of a person's death. He took the role of protector and even stood with the soul after death as a just judge and guide.'

'A just judge,' interrupted Byrd. 'How do you make that out?'

'Who's that?' said the Professor. 'I didn't know anyone else was with you, DI Wolfe.'

'DS Byrd is in the office with me.'

'Does it make a difference that I'm here?' asked Byrd.

'No, I guess not.'

'Well then please carry on.'

'Very well.'

Jo could hear the annoyance in his tone, although she was unsure as to why he'd mind Byrd being in on their conversation.

The Professor was speaking again, so Jo concentrated on his words.

'Anubis offered people the assurance that their body would be respected at death, that their soul would be protected in the afterlife, and that they would receive fair judgment for their life's work. These are the same assurances sought by people in the present day, and it is easy to understand why.'

'Excuse us for not considering our killer in that light, Professor,' said Jo. 'I can't see any good at all in what he's done to his victims.'

'If they had been free of sin, then they would have been guided to heaven.'

'Are you trying to justify our murderer's actions?' spluttered Jo.

Byrd shushed her and said, 'With all this business of cooking and eating the heart, what does that tell you?' Byrd leaned forward across the desk towards the phone.

'Anubis helped to judge the dead and he and his army of messengers were charged with punishing those who violated tombs or offended the gods. He was especially concerned with controlling the impulses of those who sought to sow disorder or aligned themselves with chaos.'

'So?' said Byrd.

'So the victims must have offended the gods, by having sinned during their lives. Don't you see that only those with the purest of souls can hope to ascend?'

'Thank you, Professor, we'll bear your insight in mind,' said Jo and cut the call.

'What was that all about?' asked Byrd. 'Why was he trying to justify Anubis' actions?'

Jo was angry with the Professor. She'd expected helpful insight from him, not tripping out information in defence of murder. Then she realised what his motive might be.

'I suspect he is trying to get more money out of us. He's paid by the number of consultations. I expect that was what he was after. Money grubbing so and so.'

'Yeah, you're probably right,' said Byrd and left the office.

# 28

Imogen Stone was in the back of an Uber trying to get to her friends who were waiting for her outside the club they liked to frequent. She grabbed her mobile as it buzzed in her pocket.

*Imogen where r u?*

*Just coming.*

*You better be we r waiting in the f \*\*cold 4 u.*

'How much longer?' she asked the driver.

'Maybe 10? Traffic's bloody awful.'

*Go in. B there soon.*

Imogen sat back and wondered what the hell she was doing, going out in the cold and dark to go to a club she'd been to many times before. The prospect didn't hold much appeal, but she'd agreed to go because she didn't want to let her friends down. While she was stuck in the back of the car she might as well check her makeup and brush her long dark hair. She wanted it to look smooth and shiny as it fell down her back.

The Uber driver was as good as his word and got her to the venue in about 10 minutes. The club was on the outskirts of Chichester, in an industrial estate of all places, but it meant there wasn't any trouble with noise abatement.

'Hey, doll,' called one of the bouncers. 'You sure looking good tonight!'

'Yeah, yeah, Clive,' Imogen retorted. 'You gonna let me in or what?'

'Be my guest,' and Clive lifted the red rope and let her through before all the poor sods in the queue. A perk of being a regular.

Inside was dark, hot and humid and Imogen made her way to the bar, where she could see one of her friends trying to buy a drink.

'Yeah! You made it,' Hazel said and flashed those hazel eyes at her friend. A corny name for sure but apparently when she was born and her parents saw those eyes, straight away they chose the name Hazel for their little girl.

'Go on, I'll get these in. My way of saying sorry. The usual?'

'Yep. Four shots of vodka,' and her friend sashayed away in time to the music.

Imogen eventually caught the eye of the barman and shouted, 'FOUR VODKA SHOTS.'

He nodded and grabbed four shot glasses from under the counter, before getting the vodka bottle. As he filled each one, he pushed them in her direction. Imogen grabbed one and drank the contents in one gulp before pushing it back at the barman. He obligingly filled it again.

After paying, Imogen tried to carry the four glasses, but could only manage three. She delivered those to her friends and went to get the last one for herself. Stood next to it and looking like the still, silent type, was a man, dressed to the latest trend. He gave Imogen a lazy smile and said, 'Okay?'

'Yes, thanks. Been in a rush and needed that.'

Imogen had to lean towards him so he could hear her over the music. The bar was some way from the DJ and the dance floor but was still too loud for normal conversation.

The man held out his hand and said, 'James.'

Imogen nodded but didn't take the proffered hand. 'Imogen.'

'Get you another?'

Imogen drank the vodka in front of her in one gulp. 'Why not,' she said and pushed her glass towards James.

'How about something cooling? Vodka and tonic?'

She smiled. 'Make it a double.'

He tipped his head in acquiescence.

Whilst her drink was being made and paid for, Imogen turned away from James and with her back to the bar watched the dance floor, which was rammed with dancers. James touched her shoulder and as she turned back, he offered her the drink.

Taking it from him she took a slurp and said, 'Fancy a dance.'

He nodded slowly, never taking his eyes from hers. 'Drink up then,' he said and she gladly obliged.

It wasn't until they were packed like sardines, dancing to the latest Calvin Harris tunes, that Imogen started to feel faint. Putting it down to the heat, she grabbed James' hand and pulled him back towards the bar.

'You okay?' he shouted in her ear.

'Yeah, just felt a bit woozy. Perhaps I should have some water.'

'Sure you don't want another vodka tonic?'

Imogen smiled at him. 'Why not. After all life's too short and all that.'

What Imogen didn't know was how prophetic those words would turn out to be.

## 29

Jo's worst fears were realised a couple of weeks later, when they found another probable victim of their killer, once again found in the water, once again wrapped in bandages. Jo and Byrd stood on the bank at Bosham looking down at the body that had just been retrieved from the water.

'It's so bloody sad, Byrd,' said Jo. 'These beautiful girls, killed, for what? Just to satisfy some psycho's perversion?'

'We don't know for sure, Boss, but yes, that's one way of looking at it.'

'It's the only one that can make any sort of sense of these senseless murders.'

'If it is Daniel Tate, Guv, then what's the fascination with Egypt about? Where has it come from?'

Jo revealed to Byrd what she'd been thinking. 'What if those books in the flat are his and he tried to hide them in Allison's room? He could have become interested in Egyptology after watching one of the documentaries that tv stations such as Channel 5 are so fond of. You know, 'Amazing new evidence from the grave of King Tut'.'

'Or, 'How the Pyramids were really built',' said Byrd.

Jo caught on, 'How did Harold Carter really die?'.

'King Tut laid Bare' is one of my particular favourites,' said Byrd and then spluttered with laughter, before remembering where he was and pulling himself together. 'Sorry, Boss,' he said sheepishly.

Jo smiled and said, 'For a moment we were enjoying ourselves there. Let's not beat ourselves up. We can't become depressed about the case, or we'll never get anything done. So, what do we know about our victim so far?'

'Judith went into the office as soon as I got the shout. She went through the missing person's report and the closest fit is a young girl called Imogen Stone.'

'What do we know about her?'

'Student at Chichester Uni studying English. Last seen on a night out in Chichester. That's all I know at the moment.'

'The university again.'

'I know, Boss.'

'But it might be a red herring.'

'Eh?'

'You know, designed to throw us off the scent. It could be a clue that just leads us down a rabbit hole.'

'Okay, but if that's the case and we ignore the university connection, where do we go from here?'

Jo swivelled to look at Byrd. 'Do you really need to ask that?'

Byrd groaned. 'Daniel Tate.'

'Exactly. Come on, there's not much we can do here. Let's go and visit our favourite suspect.'

'Yours, you mean.'

'Sorry, Byrd, did you say something?'

'No, ma'am.'

Jo's eyes flashed with anger, until she saw Byrd grinning at her. She grinned back and said, 'Let's go, Eddie.'

It took about half an hour for them to reach Daniel's flat. They made their way to his floor and Jo was just about to knock on the door when it was flung open, startling all of them.

'Bloody hell,' said Tate. 'You nearly gave me a heart attack. What the hell are you two doing here?'

'We've come to talk to you, Daniel,' said Byrd.

'What for now? Look, this is police harassment.'

'No it isn't,' said Jo, pushing past him into the flat. 'It's called a murder enquiry.'

'I've already answered all your questions.'

Daniel closed the front door and followed Jo and Byrd into the living room.

'Oh, didn't I make myself clear? It's a new murder enquiry.'

'With a new body,' said Byrd.

'Found this morning. What is her name, Byrd?'

'Imogen Stone.'

'Ah, that's right. Imogen Stone. Do you know her, Daniel?' Jo asked.

'No, I don't think so.'

'She's your type,' continued Jo. 'Tall, slim and with long dark hair.'

'What do you mean, 'my type'?'

'Alison, Charlotte and now Imogen. All three tall and slim with long dark hair. Shame you had to cut it.'

'What? What are you talking about?'

'You cut their hair to resemble an Egyptian.'

'Are you mad?'

'No, but I think you might be. What do you think, Byrd?'

103

'Oh definitely mad.'

'The only mad people here are you two,' said Tate. 'Are you going to stop talking in riddles and tell me what you want? Otherwise I'm off to work.'

'Please sit down, Mr Tate. You don't get off that easily. Byrd here has the dates we need to check your movements for.'

But in the end Jo and Eddie had no option but to let Tate go off to work. They kept him as long as they could, but he wouldn't break. Either that or he was telling the truth, said Byrd afterward and got a punch on the arm for his trouble.

Daniel Tate had kept insisting that he was in the flat, alone, exhausted after several busy days at work. When asked where he was working, he said he'd have to look in his business diary that was at the Leisure Centre. The undisputed fact was that if he was in the flat there was no one to corroborate his story. After all his flat mate, who might have been able to give him an alibi, was dead. That creeped Jo out, but it wasn't evidence, she had to admit.

## 30

Judith was pinning up details of Imogen Stone on the whiteboard when Jo and Byrd walked in from seeing Daniel Tate. They stopped to read the details and Jill joined them.

'Has she been positively identified?' Jo asked.

'Pretty much, Gov. Bill was down with the body in the morgue, so I sent him through a photograph of Imogen. He says she the spitting image of our missing girl.'

'Parents?'

'They live in the Midlands. The local police are going to see them. As Imogen was naked and wrapped in bandages and wasn't wearing any jewellery either, there's nothing that can be used for the purposes of identification. So they're arranging for her parents to come down and do a formal one.'

Jo closed her eyes for a moment. Yet another family devastated, torn apart, never to be the same again. The enormity of three dead girls was weighing heavily on her shoulders. Her first suspect, Daniel Tate, wasn't panning out and what frightened her was that she didn't have anyone else in the frame. No one at all. Anyone in Chichester could be their killer and she wouldn't know. She swayed on her feet.

Eddie must have noticed as he put out a hand to steady her. 'You alright, Boss?' he murmured.

She briefly nodded and turned to her team. 'So why all Uni victims?'

'It's a big university town. Lots of young girls around to choose from,' said Byrd.

'That's true,' said Jo. 'But it doesn't mean very much, or does it?'

'Sorry, Boss?' Jill said.

'I think there has to be other criteria as well. For instance, lots of young girls around to choose from, but they must be tall, slim, with black hair.'

'So the connection isn't necessarily the university, but it's the type that he's looking for.'

'That's right, Jill. What other connections do we have apart from looks?'

'Age? Dress?' suggested Judith, who had started noting down their discussion on the board.

'Going back to the university connection,' said Byrd, 'Is there a person they're all connected to from there?'

'Good thought,' said Jo. 'I take it you mean a professor, or Danial Tate himself.'

'That's right, Boss.'

'What about work?' said Jill. 'Do they all work part time as well as studying?'

'Great, Judith. Anyone else?'

The team shook their heads and looked around at each other.

'Okay, let's investigate those angles. Divvy up the jobs between yourselves. I'm off to see DCI Crooks who wants an update and then to the press briefing. Wish me luck, I think I'm going to need it.'

Jo left the office to calls of solidarity, knowing that

she needed all the support she could get to keep her job on this investigation. Three dead girls, at least that they knew of, and not one solid lead. It couldn't go on, she knew that. It all depended upon how generous her boss was feeling, she guessed.

# 31

Lindsay was no longer enthralled by the police press conferences. The thought of another girl taken by Anubis and subsequently found dead left her feeling strangely numb. Gone was her confidence that she could make a difference, help crack the case, use her skills to outwit the killer and help the police. Who was she kidding? Herself, that's who.

Archie noticed how despondent she was. 'Hey, Lindsay,' he said. 'What's up?'

She shook her head. 'Sorry, Archie, I'm just so sad that another girl has been found dead. Probably another student, just like me.'

'Are you feeling frightened then?'

'Yeah I guess I am.'

'Great. Write me a piece.'

'What?'

'Write me a piece on how you feel. How your friends feel. What it's like to be constantly on your guard. Scanning the crowd, trying to find someone who stands out. Someone who could be the killer. How it's driving you nuts.'

She stared at him. 'You are deadly serious?'

'Of course. Why?'

'Because that's the most awful thing you could ask me to do. Fan the fears of hundreds of innocent students. Whip up public opinion. Write it yourself!'

Lindsay gathered her stuff and stalked out of the press briefing room at the police station. She was furious. How dare he! Clattering out of the building she realised she had to do something though. Something that would help identify Anubis. She had a meeting with her tutor on Monday. Maybe he could help.

# 32

Jo returned from the press conference and a conversation with DCI Crooks, with better news than she'd originally thought she would. Calling the whole team together she confirmed they were still on the case, and that Crooks had supported them during the press conference, saying that he had absolute faith in her and her team. But afterwards she had been told in no uncertain terms by him that a result was expected in the next week or so, or otherwise another SIO would replace Jo.

'And if you're replaced?'

'We can expect most of us to be gone, Byrd.' Jo answered his question with honesty. She'd never pulled her punches with Byrd and didn't intend to start now. 'The new SIO would want his or her own team I expect.'

'Best we get on with it then,' said Judith.

'No. We are all exhausted. It's late Saturday night and I'm sending you all home. Unless we get some rest, we're never going to crack this one. We can't think straight, never mind come up with new thinking or new evidence, so that's an order. I want everyone back at 7am on Monday.'

'Does that prescription for rest extend to you, Boss?'

Jo smiled. 'Yes, Byrd it does. Now bugger off.'

With much scraping of chairs and beeping of computers, the team got ready to leave. Although Jo principally dealt with Byrd, Judith and Jill in the office, there were another 20 or so officers in the team, who carried out the leg work and the hard slog through CCTV, cold cases and missing persons. Every one of them was committed to Jo and it was her responsibility to look after them.

She went back to her office, sat at her desk, leaned back and closed her eyes. She'd go home in a minute. Have a rest and recharge, then work with her dad on the case on Sunday. That might just give her a different perspective on Tate and his antics. Waiting until everyone had gone, and the lights had been turned out, had allowed Jo a little while to force her body and mind to relax. She was ready to go home and craved the peace and quiet her little flat afforded her.

Walking to the lift she saw that Byrd was stood there waiting. For the lift? Or for her? He was dressed smart casual with his shirt sleeves rolled up to his elbows, jacket slung over his shoulder and the muddy coloured canvas trousers Jo liked so much, as it showed off his assets. She shook her head. What on earth was she thinking? It was Byrd she was talking about. Her detective sergeant. The man she worked most closely with. And perhaps that was the problem. It created a bubble around them that others had trouble breaking through. They knew each other well and could share their most outrageous thoughts about a case, without fear of being ridiculed.

Hearing her, he turned and gave her that lazy smile she knew so well. 'Hey, Boss. You okay?'

She nodded, not sure that she could speak.

'Want a drink?'

She took a deep breath and then against all her instincts, declined. 'Thanks for the offer, Eddie, but I think I should head home.'

'Family?'

'God, I hope not! I'm craving solitude not company, I'm afraid.'

The ping of the bell alerted them to the arrival of the lift, but they ignored it and walked down the stairs together. The short journey was taken in silence. As they arrived at the ground floor Byrd tried again.

'You sure about that drink?'

Jo nodded. 'I'm sure. But I appreciate the offer. See you Monday,' and walked away before she gave in to the demands of her emotions and if she was honest with herself, her body.

She had an easy journey home and as she swung her mini into the drive, she was confronted with several cars.

'Shit.' It looked like the family were there in force.

She managed to park her little car down the side of the garage and got out, hoping against hope no one would see her.

'Hi, Jo.'

She groaned. Her dad must have heard the car.

'Coming in?'

'Must I?'

'It's Kylie's birthday.'

Fuck. She forgotten all about her niece's fifth birthday. Could she really face her brothers and their wives, not to mention screaming kids?

'I can't, dad. I didn't get a present, I clean forgot about it.'

Her dad grinned. 'I knew you would, so I bought

one for you to give to her. Come in, just for a piece of cake. Please?'

'Half an hour,' Jo growled, 'and then I really will need to sleep. I suppose if I don't you won't come up and help with the case tomorrow.'

'Something like that.'

'Come on, then, let's get this over with.'

Although Jo grumbled on the surface, inside she was glad of her brothers. They'd helped her a lot in the past. And anyway, who could resist the charms of Kylie and the gap in her front teeth?

# 33

On Sunday morning Jo woke up ravenous. She'd spent an hour yesterday with the family before climbing the stairs to her flat and crashing out. The rest had done her good and she was eager to get going reviewing the case. But first she had to eat. She quickly dressed in sweats then texted her dad, asking if he wanted to join her for breakfast at a local café. His immediate reply was, 'Yes!' and by the time she reached the bottom of her stairs he'd turned up, still putting on his coat. She'd never known her dad to turn down the offer of food, hence the thickening waist. But she wouldn't mention it today. No need to spoil a nice day before it had even started.

They walked to a café about 100 yards down the road. It was an old-fashioned affair, offering cooked breakfast all day and at prices that were reasonable, but that depended upon your point of view. Jo found West Sussex to be one of the most expensive areas she'd lived in. Over £3 for a coffee was extortionate considering the small cost it took to produce.

As they entered the cafe, the smell of bacon and coffee filled Jo's nostrils and made her stomach rumble. Finding a seat near the back, Jo said, 'What do you fancy, Dad?' and grabbed a menu.

'My usual, The Full Monty.'

Jo threw him a look.

'It's the only meal I'll have today,' he protested. 'There's no plans for Sunday Lunch. Do you expect me to starve?'

Jo had to shake her head and laugh. 'No, Dad, heaven forbid I should do that.'

She ordered two Full Monty's and two coffees from a passing waitress and settled down to wait for breakfast.

'How's the case going?'

'To be honest, we're a bit stuck. Three bodies now and not a single bloody clue no matter how hard we try to find one. But I don't want to talk about it over breakfast. I'd like to enjoy my meal without thoughts of dead bodies putting me off it.'

He grinned. 'I'll second that one,' and they proceeded to talk about the family instead and the birthday they'd celebrated yesterday.


A while later, full and sleepy, they walked back to the house and up the stairs to Jo's flat. She put on more coffee to keep them awake and then took up her place in front of the board.

'The main question I have,' said Mick, 'is about Daniel Tate. Is he really our killer?'

'Bloody hell you and Byrd both. But how do I find out? Half the time he doesn't have alibis. If he's supposedly out, no one sees him. If in alone, there's no one to corroborate it, as he no longer has a flatmate.'

'What's his motive?'

'Maybe he's killed before and Alison found out about it and threaten to call the police? Is that why Alison is dead?'

'That would work, if we had any evidence of it. Are you getting any visions from him?'

'Nothing much. A feeling of danger and anger, but to be honest, it's sexual rather than homicidal.'

'Liking a bit of bondage doesn't make him a killer, Jo. Where does the Egyptian connection come from?' Mick looked as sceptical as his words.

'I've no idea,' said Jo. 'There is no evidence he's doing anything even remotely related to Egypt.'

'And the books under Alison's bed? Were they hers? Or Tate's?'

'We don't know,' admitted Jo. 'He has a connection with the Uni working in the campus gym. Maybe doing one to one training with the girls started his fantasies?'

'But what does he see in them? What makes him want to kill them? There must be something else, he can't just kill them for the sake of it. What of their traits makes him take them and want to kill them?'

'Has he been scorned by one or all of them?' mused Jo. 'Come on to them only to be rejected and now thinks they are stuck up cows? It's so hard to know what makes him tick. Maybe I need a psychological profile done on him?'

'That could be a good place to start,' agreed Mick.

Jo stood and stretched. 'Thanks for brainstorming with me, Dad.'

'I'm not so sure I helped.' Mick also stood.

'Oh yes, you always help me see the wood from the trees.'

Jo hugged him.

'So what's your next move?'

'I'm not sure yet, I'll let all this percolate and see where I am tomorrow. Oh, shit, the percolator!' and Jo ran into the kitchen, her father's laughter following her.

## 34

Jo returned to the station on Monday with a spring in her step. The rest had done her good. So had the short contact she'd had with her brothers and their families, not that she'd admit that to anyone. Then breakfast and spending the morning with her father on Sunday was another plus. She even had time for a long run on Sunday afternoon. As a result she was definitely in a better place than she had been on Saturday, when she'd felt burned out, drained and shattered.

Calling everyone together, she did her Henry V speech to the team, which had been her dad's idea. The one that gets everyone to pull together to defeat the common enemy, that together they were far stronger than their killer who was alone and that they would get the justice his victims deserved. She'd even stood on a chair to add to the effect.

'Nice one, Boss,' said Byrd afterwards, leaning on the frame of her open door.

'Thought you'd enjoy it,' she smiled. 'Anyway, what can I do for you?'

'Have you noticed Jill isn't here?'

'She isn't?'

'No. That's what I just said.'

Jo said, 'I just imagined she was hidden from my view by other officers. It never occurred to me she wouldn't be here.'

'Me neither, but she isn't. Have you heard from her?'

'No. Have you?'

'No. That's why I'm worried. It just isn't like her.'

'Have you rung her mobile?'

Byrd said, 'Yes, it just goes to answer phone and there's no reply from the land line at her flat either.'

'That's very strange.'

'I know, she appears to have disappeared into thin air.'

'Shit.'

'My thoughts exactly. At least that was my first thought.'

'Do I want to know the second?'

'Daniel Tate,' they said together.

'But why him?' Jo still wasn't too worried. The thought of Jill being taken by Daniel Tate didn't seem possible. Surely, if he was their killer, he wouldn't be so brazen as to take one of her officers. 'She's got red hair,' she finished lamely. 'How did you come to that conclusion?'

'She made some comment to me about getting one to one training from him.'

'Are you serious?'

'Yes, but I didn't think she was.'

'Fuck, Byrd, we need to find out if he's got her. One team to his flat. One to the leisure centre. Come on.'

'Are you sure?'

Jo said, 'Of course I'm bloody sure. I can't take the risk that by delaying and waiting for evidence, something might happen to her. I'd never live with myself. Come on.' Jo grabbed her suit jacket off the back of her chair and put it on as she walked out of the office.

She dispatched a team to Chichester Leisure Centre, and she went with Eddie to Daniel Tate's flat.

They screeched to a halt outside his apartment block and parked in a vague approximation of sideways onto the kerb. After running up the stairs, Jo started banging on his door, ringing the bell and making a right nuisance of herself. Eventually the door opened, and Tate stood there.

'What the hell do you two want?'

Jo didn't answer him, just barged past him into the living room. Sat on the sofa was her detective constable, Jill Sandy.

Byrd was right behind her and said, 'Bloody hell, Jill, are you alright? Has he harmed you?'

'No, Boss, why would he?'

Sauntering into the room behind them, Tate said, 'Look here, if I want to sleep with someone, why shouldn't I? Just 'cos she's one of yours.' Jo turned to find an arrogant look on his face, complete with a sly grin.

Eddie was quicker than Jo was and turned and punched Tate in the face, while Jo grabbed Jill Sandy's arm and bundled her out of the door.

'Here, that's police brutality,' shouted Tate, his hand over his nose, trying to catch the blood that was streaming out of it.

'Shut the fuck up or I'll arrest you for assaulting a police officer.'

Jo could hear the anger in Byrd's voice and had no doubt that he would take great pleasure in arresting the slimy toad that was Daniel Tate.

'I haven't touched you,' Tate grumbled, whose

shirt was now covered in blood as well as his hand.

'Not me, assaulting DC Sandy you twat.'

Jo turned to Jill who was now with her out in the hallway. 'Jill, what the fuck did you think you were doing?'

'Going undercover.'

'You blithering idiot,' Jo gasped at the ineptitude of her detective constable. 'Going under cover means the suspect doesn't know you're a police officer.'

'I just thought I might get an angle on him, you know, get inside his head.'

'The only thing he's been inside is you! Honestly you didn't need to sleep with him.'

'Sleep with him? What are you talking about?'

'Well what the hell were you doing?'

'Talking. Mostly about him. I drank too much red wine and crashed out on the sofa. He'd just woken me and was making a black coffee.'

Jo and Eddie looked at her in astonishment.

'I'm rather hurt you think I'd sleep around, Ma'am. And particularly with a suspect.'

'Jill you could have put yourself in extreme danger.'

'I'm sorry, but I don't think he's dangerous.'

'Do you have any proof of that?'

'No, not exactly.'

'Well then shut the fuck up, go home, have a shower and get changed and then come and see me in my office. Is that clear enough of an instruction for you? Oh and do not ring Daniel Tate, do not see him again, do not communicate with him in any way. Do I make myself clear?'

'Crystal, Ma'am.'

There was that m word again, which she was sure Sandy was using deliberately and it served to make Jo even angrier.

'Good, now fuck off.'

As Jill walked away from them, Jo turned on Byrd. 'Jesus, Eddie what the hell? Did you know about this?'

'Of course not, Boss. Oh and by the way…'

'Yes?'

'I love the way your eyes flash when you're angry.'

'And you can fuck off, too,' said Jo but she was smiling inside at the back handed compliment.

# 35

It was later that afternoon that Jo eventually had time for Jill Sandy. She'd seen the young constable working hard at her desk but hadn't a clue what she was doing. Whatever it was it didn't matter; she was out on her ear.

Calling her into her office, she left Jill standing in front of her desk, not asking her to sit down.

'You made a monumental mistake, DC Sandy,' she began.

'Yes, Guv.'

'What on earth possessed you?'

'This,' and she placed a folder on Jo's desk.

'What is it?'

'I'd be obliged if you'd read it before you send me back to uniform. That is what you're planning to do isn't it?'

'Damn right it is.' Jo believed in being honest with her officers, even if the truth could be seen to be harsh or extreme.

'Well, view that as mitigating circumstances.'

Jo bent her head to skim read the closely typed pages, expecting a heartfelt plea to let Sandy stay on the team. But she soon stopped, went back to the beginning and began to read properly.

Well I'll be buggered she thought, for Sandy had written a psychological profile of Daniel Tate.

'That's why I went to his flat. Not to sleep with him, but to find out what makes him tick for you.'

'How the hell do you know about all this stuff.'

'I'm doing an OU degree in psychology, Guv. Paying for it myself and doing it in my own time. I'll go and collect my things now. I'd like to thank you – '

'Oh shut up will you. Tell Byrd to come in here and you can go and see Judith and see what she'd like you to do next.'

'Oh. Right. Yes. Thank you.'

'That means go now, DC Sandy, before I change my mind.'

'I'm gone,' she called from the door and Jo watched her fairly skip over to Judith's desk.

Jo had seen Byrd watching the exchange and he sauntered over to Jo's door.

'Is she out?'

'No.'

'How come?'

'Read this,' said Jo and pushed the file folder across her desk to Byrd. 'Sandy reckons our killer is schizophrenic with delusions.'

'Bloody hell,' said Eddie, picking up the folder.

'And she reckons it's not Daniel Tate, because he is a narcissist.'

Sitting down opposite Jo he started to read.

# 36

Lindsay had felt much better since her meeting with her tutor. She'd told him where the police investigation was at and then what Archie had proposed she do and how cross she was with him for it. To her surprise her tutor had sided with Archie. He'd said the reporter had a point and surely Jo could think about things from that angle. He'd reminded her it was still within the remit of forensic psychology to understand how the victims and the general public felt, as well as helping to identify perpetrators from an understanding of their psyche.

He'd also suggested she investigate the Anubis angle further. He'd decided it would help her to get a more in-depth feeling for the Egyptian God. To that end he was organising a meeting for her with an Egyptology professor in the History Faculty. He'd stressed upon her that the secret of a good dissertation was in-depth analysis coupled with original thinking.

She was sat in the window of Costa Coffee, slowly stirring her drink and waiting for Archie. She'd arranged to meet him so she could apologise. She'd even written the bare bones of the article for him by way of an olive branch.

She wondered which Professor her tutor would arrange for her to see. She pulled out of her bag a printout of the Faculty staff she'd taken from the university website. She looked at each one in turn and wondered if she was going to be lucky enough to meet with Professor Russell. Now there was a horny looking bloke, despite his age.

# 37

*Anubis was beginning to feel uncomfortable. He kept having feelings that someone was watching him. Following him. He started to take notice of people around him. Who was it? A friend of one of those he'd already taken? Someone upset by his choice of victim? The police?*

*The trouble was there was nothing he could put his finger on. He would scan a crowd when the back of his neck started to prickle, but not see a familiar face. Every now and then he saw a shadow pass him by.*

*He'd taken to turning the lights off at home and peering through the curtains to check the road outside, searching for cars with people in that could be putting him under surveillance.*

*Was it the police?*

*A member of the public?*

*He supposed that if it was the police, they would have a pool of people they could call upon, meaning he wouldn't keep seeing the same faces in the crowd, or in a café, or the local supermarket. He'd taken to looking all around him, at all times. Never really able to settle. It was unnerving. He kept reminding himself*

*that he was Anubis. The God of Death. No one would*
*dare move against him.*
  *But it seemed that someone was.*
  *Someone was getting far too close.*
  *For that they'd have to pay.*


Jo and Byrd were stood looking at the board. On it were photographs of Daniel Tate, leaving the flat, arriving at work, working with a client, taking a class, walking home, all taken at some point during his days. But not one showed any suspect activity.

'What about his alibis, Byrd?'

'Doesn't really have any, Guv.'

'See that's the trouble isn't it? Daniel Tate doesn't have an alibi for any of the nights we think the girls were taken. Not even for several days either side.'

'I know what you mean,' said Byrd. 'Sometimes he says he was out, but he can't be found on CCTV. At other times he says he was in, but as he's now home alone there is no one to corroborate his story, after all his flat mate, Alison, is dead.'

'That's what creeps me out about him.' Jo sat down and took of her heels, massaging her feet. She'd been on them for far too long. God knows why she'd put them on this morning. Just fancied a change, she supposed. But she was paying for it now.

Byrd persisted, 'But that is not evidence is it?'

'No but I want him brought here and I'm going to hold him for a while, let him sweat it out. That will show him I mean business.'

'Look, are you sure, Jo?'

Byrd had just used her name at work, something he rarely did. 'Of course I am,' she snapped. 'What's your problem?' She quickly replaced her shoes and stood. She didn't like being intimidated by Byrd standing over her.

'There's just no evidence to suggest that he's our killer. You know that, deep down, don't you?'

'Byrd,' Jo warned.

'And Jill's profile concludes that he's narcissistic, but not necessarily a psychopath. So I don't get it.'

'Get what?'

'Where your obsession comes from.'

'Obsession? Jesus, Byrd, you're really outdoing yourself this time, aren't you? What makes you think you can say anything you like to me? I'm your superior officer and you will show me some respect!'

'Respect has to be earned, Jo.'

'What the fuck? Jesus. I never thought that you of all people would speak to me like this. I've no idea what's going on in your head, but whatever it is, it doesn't allow you to talk to me this way.'

Jo stormed into her office and grabbed her handbag.

'I'm going home before either of us do or say something we'll regret. And I think you need to adjust your thinking by the time you come into the office tomorrow. Either that, or you're out. Do I make myself clear?'

'Perfectly, Ma'am.'

The use of 'ma'am' made her even crosser, as Byrd turned on his heel and made for the stairs. Jo walked to the lifts, taking deep breaths that didn't help bring her anger level down one bit. She didn't want to take the lift but wasn't about to use the stairs as that's where Byrd had gone. Once in her car, she set the engine into sports mode and raced out of the car park, heading for home.

The twenty-minute journey was achieved in ten and Jo sent the gravel on the drive flying as she pulled up in front of the garage. She ran up the stairs, slammed the door shut behind her and grabbed a beer.

She'd only taken one gulp of the drink, when there was a buzz from her door. She walked over to the intercom and said, 'Look, leave me alone, I'm not in the mood, Dad.'

'It's not your dad, Jo, it's me.'

'Oh, Byrd.' Jo thought about not letting him in, but in the end pressed the unlock button.

She didn't speak when he arrived at the top of her stairs. She was still too upset with him and felt the safer action would be to keep her mouth shut. There was ice forming around her heart and it was growing in thickness as she realised that Byrd had not turned out to be the man she thought he was.

'You've got some nerve showing up here.'

'Yeah, well I fancied a beer,' and Byrd walked over to the fridge and helped himself.

'What the fuck do you think you're doing? You rip me to shreds at work and now walk around my flat as though you own the place. I think you'd better go. I've had quite enough of you for one day.'

'No.'

'What? What do you mean, no?'

Jo walked over to Byrd, who put his beer on the kitchen worktop, and she started to try and push him out of the flat, with both hands on his chest.

'Go on, get out of here.'

But Byrd didn't move, and Jo realised that he was stronger than she was. She was trying to regulate her breathing with little success. She was in danger of having a panic attack. She just couldn't believe that Byrd would treat her like this.

'I'm not leaving, Jo. I'm not leaving you.'

'Get out of here,' she screamed, hating herself for reacting like this.

'Stop pushing me away. Emotionally I mean. You don't need to be so frosty. Hiding your true feelings.'

And then, instead of leaving, Byrd pressed her up against the wall, his body moulding to hers. He grabbed her wrists and held them above her head. Jo started to feel something. Was it fear? She wasn't sure. It was something. But not something bad. Not threatening. Not frightening in one sense, but bloody petrifying in another…

His lips on hers meant the rest of that thought blew away.

Once the shock subsided, she realised she was rather enjoying it.

And that she had waited such a long time for it.

Her anger quickly turned to passion as they kissed again.

## 38

The buzzing of Byrd's phone woke Jo, and she found she had slept with her limbs wound around him.

Dear God, what have I done?

I've just had the night of my life, that's what.

Jo had thought it would just be sex, not mean anything, never to be repeated, but it turned out to be so much more than that. Not that she was going to admit any of that to Byrd. And the never to be repeated rule still applied. Didn't it? But she'd slept. No dreams. No nightmares. Just sweet restorative sleep. The sleep of contentment.

Her own phone buzzing made her turn away from him and grab it off the bedside table. Byrd had woken as well and was kissing her arm, her shoulder, her neck. Jo groaned as her body started to respond to the kisses, so she put the phone back down and gave in to Byrd's insistent probing, kissing and kneading. For the first time in her life she didn't leap out of bed to rush to work. She was sure they had a few extra minutes...

Afterwards she rang Judith back. 'Yes? You wanted me?'

'Morning, Boss. Got a new missing person. Could

be Anubis' next victim.'

Jo sat up, the bed sheet falling away from her naked body.

'Who? Where? When?'

'I'll text you the details. Oh and have you any idea where Byrd is, Boss?'

'Byrd?'

'Yes, Boss, you know, Detective Sergeant Eddie Byrd. I can't find him, to let him know.'

'Just send him a text, Judith. I'm sure he'll see it soon. In the meantime, I'll get there as quickly as I can.'

Maybe they shouldn't have taken those few extra minutes she told Byrd and leapt out of bed to grab the fastest shower ever, quickly followed by her DS.

Jo looked down at the photograph of the possible next victim of the killer they'd dubbed Anubis. Well strictly speaking it was the Chichester Argus that had coined the name and Jo and her team had adopted it.

Was Lindsay Hutt his next victim? Lindsay was also studying at Chichester Uni, but this time working towards a degree in criminology. Did that mean anything? Jo left her office to find Eddie and see what he thought.

'Yes, Boss?' he asked as she walked up to his desk, his eyes shining with a secret smile. As they'd parted earlier, on the steps of her flat, they'd agreed not to mention what had just happened to anyone. And preferably not even themselves. It wasn't a good idea for it to carry on, because damnit they worked together. Jo was his senior officer. It was a can of worms that should stay firmly closed.

'She's studying criminology,' she said.

'Who? Lindsay?'

'Yeah. I'm just wondering if that means anything?'

'Best we go and find out.'

'Go?'

'To her room. It will give us a sense of who she is.'

'Absolutely. Sure.'

In Byrd's car, sat in the passenger seat as he drove, Jo was acutely aware of him. She became fascinated by his hands, strong and firm on the wheel, that a short time ago had been exploring her body. The rippling of the muscles in his arm as he changed gear. His breathing making his chest rise and fall as it had done last night, when she'd laid her head on his chest and he had tucked his arm around her, holding her close. Keeping her safe.

Stopping at a set of traffic lights, he turned to look at her.

'Boss.'

'Byrd.'

They spoke together.

'About last night,'

'Look, last night.'

They did again and then laughed.

'It was good though, wasn't it?' Byrd had that twinkling thing going on in his eyes again.

'Hell, yes,' said Jo, biting her bottom lip with her teeth and feeling far younger than her years. Wait, was she blushing? Dear God, this had to stop! 'Not to be spoken of.'

'Not at work,' Byrd agreed, causing Jo to laugh.

'I meant ever!'

'No you didn't.'

The lights turned green and he drove away a smile playing across his lips. No more was said and soon they pulled up opposite Lindsay's shared house.

Jo introduced them to the man who answered the door. 'Do you live here?'

'Nah, just visiting, like. I'm just off,' and he pushed past Jo and Byrd, a waft of weed emanating from his clothes.

A girl came clattering down the stairs and said, 'Oh thank goodness you've come! I'm so worried about Lindsay.'

'Did you report her missing?'

'Yes, I'm Hayley Short. Is there any news?'

'Not yet. It's early days.'

'Yes. Sorry.'

'Can we see Lindsay's room first, please?'

'Sure,' and she led them round to the back of the house. 'Lindsay's room has the view of the back garden. Luckily her door wasn't locked, so when I got no reply to my knock this morning, I was able to open it and saw that she wasn't in. The patio doors were open, but I closed them as the wind and rain was coming in.'

'Thanks,' said Jo. 'We'll come and find you when we've finished.'

'What? Oh yes, sorry,' and Hayley backed out of the room.

Jo and Byrd looked around them in silence. It was a large room, with light flooding in from the patio doors. It clearly used to be a sitting room, or dining room, that the landlord had turned into an extra bedroom. A trick used to maximise the rental income from the house. But what really caught their attention were the cork boards on each wall. Pinned to them was stuff about the case. Newspaper cuttings, photographs, maps, bits of string looped around some of the pins which seemed to indicate possible connections with the case and lastly a myriad of images of some of the notable Egyptians including Anubis.

'Bloody hell,' said Byrd. 'It looks like she was trying to solve the case all on her own!'

'Doesn't it just,' agreed Jo. 'We need to find her. Anubis could be keeping her somewhere, but where? I want lots of eyes on CCTV, perhaps we can trace her movements.'

'I'll get Bill to send a forensic team over here. It looks as if an intruder came through the patio doors and quite possibly attacked her.'

'Get him to fingerprint Hayley also,' she said. 'Bill will need them for elimination.'

'Will do, Boss.'

Byrd reached for his phone while Jo went to find Hayley.

## 39

'Hayley?' Jo called as she left Lindsay's room.

'Yes?' Hayley appeared from the front of the house.

'Can I ask you some questions?'

'Yes, of course, come through to the kitchen.'

Hayley cleared a space at the kitchen table for Jo. Not that the surface she revealed could be described as clean. There were many rings from hot mugs with various unidentified splodges marring the tabletop. This had clearly been a student house for many years. Wallpaper was beginning to peel off the walls where they met the ceiling. A large, but old fridge, churned away in the corner of the kitchen and the top of the cooker held stains from a myriad of meals. Jo hoped the chair she'd sat on was clean as she had a new trouser suit on. It was a deep plum colour, that she'd bought on a whim from her local charity shop, brand new with the tags still on it. Jo was a fully paid up member of the charity shop ethos of recycle, recycle, recycle, but was very picky about what she bought.

'Do you want any tea or coffee?' Hayley was saying. 'Mind you I don't think there's any milk.'

'No, you're fine.' Jo felt it was more than her life was worth to drink anything produced in that kitchen. 'I take it you've contacted all Lindsay's friends?'

'Yes. I've not seen her since, oh, two nights ago when she went out to meet a local newspaper reporter. She said it was something to do with her course. The next morning she wasn't in her room, so, well, I guessed she'd hit it off with him, know what I mean?'

Jo smiled in response and tried hard not to blush as images of last night when she'd hit it off with Byrd flashed in her head.

'But then I got calls saying that she hadn't been at Uni yesterday and did I know if she was okay? Well, no I didn't know. But I thought she'd be back at some point last night. But when I got up this morning, there was still no sign of her, and her room was just like she left it. She's not answering calls or texts to her mobile.'

'Have the patio doors been open all this time?'

'Yes I'm pretty sure they have.'

'So someone could have entered her room from the garden?'

'Yes, I suppose. I only closed them this morning because of the weather. Do you think someone got in and took her? Oh my God! I'm sorry I just didn't think.'

'Now, now, Hayley, let's not jump to conclusions. What was Lindsay wearing when you last saw her?'

'You mean when she went to meet that bloke?'

'Yes. I want to track her movements on CCTV.'

'Well she was wearing jeans, of course. A baggy beige jumper that was one of her favs. Her Uni scarf and flat brown boots.'

'Thanks a lot. Do you have a recent photo?'

'Yes, we took some last week.'

'Send them to my phone, would you?' and Jo gave Hayley her mobile number.

Back at the office Jo had no alternative but to wait for the CCTV operatives to do their thing. They knew far more about following people on the system than she did, so was told to butt out and leave them alone. The objective was not just to track Lindsay's movements, but also to see if they could spot anyone stalking her.

Walking back to her office, she met Byrd and told him to interview Daniel Tate.

'Not Tate again, Jo. Do I have to?'

'Yes you do,' she snapped, 'and it's Boss or Guv while we're at work. And no lip either.'

'Ah so I've the green light to do the opposite when we're not at work, do I?'

'Fuck me, Byrd. Shut up and get on with it!'

'Gladly, Boss,' he breathed into her ear.

Jo's cheeks flamed, but she couldn't berate him as she'd walked right in to that one!

Jo was prowling around the office when Byrd got back.

'Bloody hell, you took your time!'

'Sorry, Boss. The staff at the Leisure Centre weren't much help and it took me a while to find him. They're probably as pissed off as I am about all this.'

'Byrd, all I'm interested in is where the fuck was Daniel Tate the night Lindsay went missing.'

'He had a date.'

'You what?'

'He had a date and no ordinary one, but a double date with a friend, so he isn't likely to get three people to lie for him, now is he? They went to an Indian in town, so he'll also be on CCTV. Then last night he had a friend over, and they played computer games until gone midnight.'

'Do you have details of these friends of his?'

'Of course, Boss.'

'Well bloody ring them, then. Oh and after that get CCTV to pick him up leaving the restaurant and let's see where he went.'

'Yes, Boss,' Eddie said and turned away from her. Jo felt disgusted with herself. One for being so harsh to poor Byrd and secondly for having, yet again, to face her obsession with Daniel Tate, which everyone apart from her seemed to think was misplaced. For the first time, Jo began to feel a prickle of unease over the choice of her first suspect.

# 40

That night, her father went over in response to her plea, asking him to help her decide what to do next.

'So you're having problems with your suspect, are you?' he said as he huffed up the stairs. 'Bloody hell, Jo, we'll have to put in a stair lift soon.'

That made Jo laugh. He was just kidding around to lighten her mood.

'So, here's my problem,' she began. 'We've had a 4th abduction. Or at least we think we have.'

'Okay,' he said, reading the new information Jo had pinned to her wall. 'Another Uni girl?'

'Yeah. We went to her house today.'

'Anything?'

'No, I didn't get anything from the room, nor from any of her stuff. I think at this stage she's just abducted and not yet dead.'

'Okay… It makes sense that our killer is someone with a connection to the university.'

'Tate has, Dad, he works at the gym on campus.'

Her father nodded. 'Fair enough. Does he have an alibi for the night she went missing?'

'Yes.'

'Sorry?'

'I said, yes he does.'

'That's the first time it's happened.'

'Right.'

'Can it be broken? Proven to be false?'

'Nah, Byrd contacted them all.'

'All?'

'Yes, three friends from the date with him on the night Lyndsay went missing and a fourth from the following night. If I can't pin the fourth girl on him, then how would he have done the first three, but not the fourth? I wondered about a copycat for the latest one?'

'Doesn't make much sense really, Jo, does it? These abductions need to be meticulously planned. Are you sure your killer is Tate? I mean, really sure?'

Her dad wasn't the first man to ask her that. To question her choice of suspect. Thoughts of Byrd sent her into a daydream of what had happened last night in this very flat.

'Jo?'

Bloody hell, her dad had been talking and she missed it completely. 'Sorry, dad, what?'

'I was musing again that the abductions and then killings had to be meticulously planned. They weren't spur of the moment crimes. Anubis knew the girls and probably followed them for quite a while before he took them.'

'That's it!' Jo shouted.

'What?'

'Meticulously planned. I need to go back to Lindsay's street, show the students she shares a house with and their immediate neighbours, a photo of Tate, to see if anyone has seen him hanging around.' She grabbed her bag and car keys and ran down the stairs. There was no time like the present.

# 41

Jo was in Lindsay's street in Chichester within 15 minutes. She checked with the occupants of the house that were in. Had they seen anyone acting suspiciously? Did they recognise Jo's picture of Daniel Tate? But nothing.

Then she tried the house next door. Nothing.

In desperation she knocked on the three doors either side. But still nothing. Until she tried the house on the corner.

The girl who came to the door was bundled up in pyjamas and a dressing gown. She didn't recognise Daniel Tate. But then said, 'I know the other bloke, though.'

'Which one?'

'The one in the paper.'

'Sorry?'

'Hang on a minute.' The girl scrabbled through papers strewn all over a hall table. 'Here,' she said and thrust it at Jo. The newspaper was open to a photo of the professor they'd contacted from the University. Professor Russell. It seemed he was helping the press with information about Egyptology, which the newspaper reported was also connected to the murders.

The girl was still talking, and Jo had to tear her eyes away from the newspaper and focus on what was being said. 'Sorry. What?'

'I saw him waiting for Lindsay a couple of times,' she said.

'Waiting? Was she seeing him then?'

'No idea. But he was there.'

'Where?'

She pointed to the opposite side of the street. 'Under that lamp post.'

'So he could have been following her, not necessarily meeting her,' mused Jo.

'I guess. Anyway hope that helped?'

'Yes, yes, thanks very much. It did,' and Jo hurried back to her car.

# 42

The next morning she received a phone call from the office. It was 7 am and she'd just stepped out of the shower. Dripping all over the carpet, she heard she was summoned to see DCI Crooks at 8am. Not asked. Ordered. Shit.

After quickly drying herself and dressing, she clipped up her damp hair, grabbed her bag and keys and raced for the car.

She made it with one minute to spare.

Crooks made her stand throughout the interview.

'Well, Jo. What do you make of the case so far?' Friendly enough words but delivered with a steely menace. Sarcasm in there somewhere as well.

'I've just got a new lead, Boss,' she said. And proceeded to tell him about her canvassing Lindsay's neighbours last night and finding that Professor Russell had been watching her.

'And you think this is worth following up?'

'Most definitely, Boss,' she said.

'As long as this actually pans out and you don't waste even more time chasing down an innocent suspect.'

'Boss.'

To be honest Jo couldn't think of anything else to say. Her cheeks flamed and she looked down at her shoes. Why the hell did Crooks always make her feel like a recalcitrant schoolgirl in the headmaster's office, instead of an intelligent woman and a damn good DI.

'Go and get on with it then and stop wasting time here.'

'Boss.'

Jo turned and fled before he could change his mind.

Once in the stairwell on the way to the Major Crimes Unit, Jo sat on a step and tried very hard not to cry. To cry was to show weakness. And she was not weak. Most definitely not. No one who knew what she'd gone through to get well, could ever think that. She knew it was Crooks' role to be the big bad boss at times (big, bad wolf) and she could live with that. Deciding not to take criticism to heart, but to use it to forge ahead, she stood and ran down the last few steps to her office.

She called for Eddie. 'Byrd, we need to go back to the beginning with the case.'

'What the fuck, Guv?'

Jo went on to tell him about the sighting of the Professor waiting outside Lindsay's house and the stay of execution she'd negotiated with Crooks. 'So, let's go back to the beginning. I want to go back to Alison Rudd's flat.'

'Not Daniel Tate again!'

'No, not this time. I want to see Alison's room once more, before her parents strip it and sell the flat.'

'OK you're the boss,' he huffed.

'For the moment, Byrd. Only for the moment. So you better ring Tate and get him or a neighbour to let us in.'

Tate had left a key with a neighbour in case of inadvertently locking himself out, so all it took was a phone call from him and a knock on the door of the neighbour. While Byrd was assuring the woman that they would return the key to her very soon and that they really were the police, Jo was already letting herself into the flat.

It had that stale, male smell about it, now that Alison was no longer there. It made Jo want to throw open the windows, but she resisted and went into Alison's room, stopping at the door and taking her time to look around. It was pretty much as they'd left it, apart from all the liberally applied black fingerprint powder.

Thrown on her bed were the two books on Egyptology. Byrd arrived and stood near her. She could feel his breath on her neck. It made her want to melt. Instead she took a step into the room to put distance between them.

'Didn't we see these books the first time we were here?' she asked him.

'Yes, why?'

'Did anyone open them?'

'No idea, Guv.'

'Did you?'

'Nah.'

'Neither did I.' She picked up the two books and opened them. 'Well we should have.'

'Why?'

'These are from the Chichester University Library.'

'What?' he grabbed the books from her to look himself.

'Find out if Alison was doing a course there. Unless we've already checked that?' But even as she asked the question, she was pretty sure she knew the answer.

'Don't think so, Boss. We figured there was no

need. She worked full time. She wasn't a student. Never thought she had anything to do with the Uni. Assumed, you know?'

'Unfortunately assuming doesn't get to the truth, does it? And it means I could have made a very big mistake.'

# 43

They had only been back at the office about 15 minutes before the front desk rang Jo.

'Um, Ma'am there's a Daniel Tate here to see you.'

Jo frowned. 'We don't have an appointment.'

'He's insisting I'm afraid. To be honest, he's in a bit of a state and causing quite a disruption with his ranting and raving.'

'Oh God, I'll be there in a minute.'

Jo put the phone down and took a few deep breaths. She'd been trying to avoid the awful thought that perhaps she'd been wrong about Daniel Tate. And now he was here. Oh well, she'd better face him.

'Byrd,' she called. 'Daniel Tate's in reception being rather vocal and demanding to see me.'

'Not on your own, he's not,' and Byrd put down his own phone and stood and joined her in the short journey downstairs. Eddie occasionally touched her back as he guided her. Jo noticed, but pretended she hadn't, as she rather liked it and didn't want him to stop.

They heard Tate before they saw him. 'Get that bitch down here, now!'

'The Detective Inspector is on her way, I've told you that, Mr Tate.'

'Don't fucking Mr Tate me!'

The rest of the tirade was cut off as Jo and Byrd emerged into the lobby. Byrd took the lead.

'What's this all about, Daniel?'

Tate pointed at Jo. 'That bitch, that's what this is all about.'

'If you'll calm down, we can go to an interview room and talk about it. Yes?'

'Oh, listen to him, I'm in the wrong, again! Why can't you lot get off my back for once? You've destroyed my life and all you can say is 'calm down Mr Tate'. You're a joke, a fucking joke!'

Tate didn't even see the Desk Sergeant coming, he was so focused on Byrd and Jo. In an instant he was slammed into the wall and put in handcuffs before he could finish his next expletive.

'Thank you,' said Byrd. 'Mr Tate, shall we?' and Tate was ushered through the door and into an interview room, where he was placed in a chair, hands still cuffed.

Jo and Byrd followed him in.

'Aren't you going to take these off?'

'Not until I know you'll behave,' said Byrd. 'So, come on, we're here. What do you want to say to us?'

All the fight had gone from Tate and Jo was shocked to see him in tears. Jo and Byrd sat down opposite him.

Will you take these off?'

'Not yet. Just talk, Daniel, spit it out.'

The upshot was that Tate had been sacked from both gyms. So not only was his flat mate murdered, but he'd lost his jobs and was about to be made homeless. No private clients would touch him with a bargepole. All the women thought he would hurt them, and the men just thought he was scum. People he considered as his friends hadn't stood by him and everyone seemed to be looking at him with suspicion in their eyes.

'I can't take much more of this,' he finished. 'My doctor says I'm having a nervous breakdown. I'm going back home to Reading. But my dad's appalled at what I've been accused of and it's broken my mum's heart that people think her only son is a killer. And not just a killer but a serial killer!'

The volume of Tate's voice was increasing once more and Byrd growled at him to shut up, or he'd end up in a cell.

Jo was wanting to say sorry to Tate, but the words kept getting stuck. Her throat was working but nothing was coming out. She was appalled. Had her behaviour really taken this young man to the edge of his sanity? Had she nearly destroyed him because she felt she was so right, but in fact had been completely wrong?

Tate was now slumped in his chair, tears dripping onto his legs. 'My dad is coming to collect me tomorrow morning, so I'm going home to pack. He said I had to come and ask if I could go with him to Reading, or if I had to stay within the confines of Chichester until you'd finished your enquiries?'

Byrd made to speak, but Jo put her hand over his to stop him.

'If you'll leave your contact details with the desk sergeant you can go, Mr Tate. I have no objection to you going to Reading. And now we really must get on.'

Jo's chair scraped as she stood.

'And is that it?' Daniel looked incredulous. 'No apology? Nothing?'

'I'm afraid that until our enquiries are complete, you will continue to be a suspect.'

Byrd kicked her foot. She glanced at him to see he was encouraging her to say more.

She cleared her throat, 'But we have reason to believe there may be another party involved. If that theory turns out to be correct, then I shall apologise to you personally. Thank you for coming in.'

Jo practically ran for the door. While Byrd spoke to the Desk Sergeant, Jo dashed into the stairwell. Byrd found her shortly after that, taking deep breaths and trying to get her emotions under control.

'You okay, Boss?'

She nodded. He sat down beside her on the cold concrete steps, put his arm around her and drew her into his chest. It was that simple, compassionate act that broke her.

With her tears wetting his shirt, she said, 'Dear God, Eddie. What the hell have I done?'

# 44

Jo was stood by the incident board and began telling the team that one of Lindsay's neighbours had said they'd seen Professor Russell outside Lindsay's house. They had also confirmed that the books Alison had on Egyptology were hers from Chichester University library. Now Jo wanted to know where they were to date.

'Okay, team, what have we got?''

Judith spoke first. 'I've confirmed that Alison Rudd was an OU student doing a strand on Egyptology towards a history degree.'

'Was Professor Russell her tutor?'

'No, but that means nothing. She was in the history department. She had books from the university library.'

'Guv, he did a guest lecture,' Sandy came rushing up. 'I've checked and Alison attended it, so the Prof had seen her, at the very least. Remember she was a very striking girl. She already had that Egyptian type haircut going on, so he'd be drawn to her.'

'Okay, but just like Daniel Tate, none of this new information proves anything.'

'It could take the investigation on a different path.'

'I know that, Sandy, thank you.'

Jo ran her hand over her face in an effort to encourage herself to keep awake and keep going. But it seemed Byrd had noticed how tired she was.

'Look, Guv, let's call it a night,' he said. 'We're all too tired to think straight and we're going to make mistakes.'

Unusually, Jo agreed. Even though she was driven, she wasn't stupid and realised that she was beginning to suffer from brain fog. 'You're right,' she nodded. 'OK 8 am tomorrow. We'll have a run through the case and then think about having the Prof brought in for questioning once we have our ducks in a row.'

Everyone started packing up and Jo went into her office and slumped in her chair. She needed a drink. A white wine and soda with lots of ice would go down really well about now. Then her stomach rumbled, reminding her that she hadn't eaten all day.

Picking up her mobile, she called her dad. 'Do you want a Chinese?'

'Oh yes please,' he was quick to agree.

'And a run through of the case?'

'Of course!'

'Great, thanks, Dad. I'm just leaving now and will pick up a takeaway on the way. I should be there in about 30 minutes.'

'I'll listen out for you,' Mick said as Jo killed the call.

She grabbed her handbag and filled it with her mobile phone and her keys and the folder containing the up to date photocopies for her board at home.

Looking around she saw that everyone had gone as she'd told them to. Including Byrd. She wasn't sure how she felt about that. Disappointed? Relieved? A little lonely? She supposed she would have liked to find him waiting for her. But he wasn't. Maybe what had happened the other night didn't matter to him. But then again, he had sat on the steps with her earlier today, giving her a hug when she most needed it.

For God's sake, she thought. Pull yourself together woman! Grabbing her bag she hurried out of her office. She'd never defined herself by what a man may think of her and she wasn't about to start now. She was a Detective Inspector for God's sake and she hadn't got there by having liaisons with other officers. She'd got there all on her own, with lots of hard work. Oh and support from her dad, of course. He was the only man she relied on and she intended to keep it that way.

Didn't she?

# 45

Once in her car Jo drove off, then about five miles later pulled into the kerb to park near their favourite Chinese take-away. She was just climbing out of the car when she saw the Egyptology professor coming out of the shop. She stayed where she was, partially hidden by her car door. She realised that he was a way away from his home and wondered why he was purchasing food in this small residential area.

The more she thought about it, the conundrum became an itch that she had to scratch and as he drove away, she made the split-second decision to follow him.

*Big, bad wolf.*

Climbing back in her car she quickly did a u turn in the street.

She stayed a few cars back from him, which was easy in the Chichester suburbs, but not so much when she realised he was heading for the basin and Bosham. By now Jo was convinced she had done the right thing by following him. She was excited by the prospect of finding out more about the professor, where he went and who he met.

When he turned off onto a single-track road which seemed to end at a house in the near distance, she parked and killed the engine. Climbing out she wondered if it really was going to be that easy? She wasn't sure.

She cautiously made her way down the lane to the house. A thin mist was collecting in pockets, making her shiver with cold as she walked through them. She felt drawn to the house (big, bad wolf) she could see intermittently through the mist. What if he had someone there? Maybe the latest victim, Lindsay, was still alive? What if she was there in that house? Jo continued her clandestine journey. She was sure the team had checked out this derelict house weeks earlier and then dismissed it as empty and not relevant, when they'd done an extensive search of old buildings near the river that she'd ordered after having her vision. Well it felt bloody relevant now, she decided. It was close to the part of Bosham where they'd found the bodies and yet was isolated and no one would really take a second look at it. It was just another part of the river that had fallen into disuse and disrepair.

She didn't know if Anubis owned the house or was just using it as his lair. Well she guessed she'd soon find out. She paused, hidden by a clump of bushes and watched the house for a while. She couldn't see the Professor. He'd disappeared into the bowels of the building. She couldn't see any lights in any of the windows. There was no door, as it had rotted away over the years and most of the windows were smashed, no doubt by local youths having their bored fun. It would be an unsuitable building for Anubis' lair with no electricity and no protection from the weather. Still he'd disappeared into it, so she had to investigate.

Moving silently through the long grass she approached the building. Moving slightly to the left, she reached the old house and leaned with her back against the wall by the doorway. All was quiet and still. Only the mist was moving. Tendrils were swirling around the doorway as if inviting her in. Taking a deep breath she turned and stood in the doorway.

She knew it would take a few minutes for her eyes to adjust to the darkness inside the building and that for a few moments she would be blind. What she didn't expect was some kind of shock to her chest. She heard faint crackles that sounded like lightening, before falling to the floor unconscious.

# 46

'We're in trouble now.'

'I know that, bloody shut up!'

Anubis knew full well that the police were after him when Jo Wolfe turned up. But it didn't mean to say they knew where he was, otherwise they would have already stormed the house. He could be confident they knew nothing. Not even that DI Wolfe was missing yet. So he reckoned he'd be alright for a bit.

What bothered him was how Jo had realised who he was. If she could work it out then her team would draw the same conclusion. Wouldn't they? Either that or they'd find her car. He'd have to move it when he could.

'How are you going to deal with them both? You're in danger, I tell you.'

'I have my trusty prod to keep them under control. They will be grovelling at my feet before long, begging to be allowed to live. Trying to convince me not to hurt them.'

'Oh well, if you say so.'

'I do, so fuck off and leave me alone to think.'

Anubis decided he would take Lindsay first. She'd

*been there the longest. He'd not had much time to play with her and wanted to change that.*

*Both women made him very angry, though. Both investigating him. Granted it was DI Wolfe's job, but Lindsay? She had made a point of singling him out. Gone to the local paper and working with their reporter. Using her criminology course to help her investigate the case. He'd been furious when her tutor had approached him and asked if he would talk to Lindsay about Egyptology, to help her investigation. Once that happened, he knew that she could sink him. Knew that he couldn't let her live.*

*He'd watched her for a couple of days and then he pounced. It was so easy! Fancy sleeping with the patio doors unlocked. She was asking for trouble. He'd not had to pick the lock; the door had just opened under his hand. A couple of prods disabled her and then it was a simple matter of slinging her over his shoulder and carrying her away through the garden and over the fence.*

*She wanted to know about Anubis, did she?*

*Well it was about time for her education to begin.*

Jo slowly came round. Her chest felt as though it were on fire and she wondered if her heart had been damaged, or stopped, or skipped a beat. She knew worrying was a useless activity. She had to concentrate on the here and now. Where was she? She groaned as she went to sit up and was shocked to hear a woman's voice.

'Oh, thank goodness you're alright.'

As Jo's eyes adjusted to the gloom, she realised the girl talking to her was the missing victim, Lindsay.

'Oh, Lindsay! How are you?' asked Jo. 'We've been looking everywhere for you.'

'We?'

'Sorry, I'm Jo Wolfe, Chichester Police. Not that that will do us much good. No one knows I'm here!'

Jo looked around the room. The floor was soil, the walls bare brick and there was a low wattage light bulb over the door. No windows. No noises. It looked like her vision, looking into the abyss, had been right. Not that she'd ever doubted it. The problem with her visions was that she didn't always know what they meant at the time. Well, now she bloody well did!

She didn't think she'd been injured, just stunned. Looking down she saw her new suit was now filthy and was that rips on her trousers? Pushing aside stupid thoughts about her clothing, she took a closer look at Lindsay and saw that Anubis had already cut her hair.

'Do you know who he is?' Jo had to ask.

'No, he always wears that wolf's head thing and never speaks.'

'Maybe he never speaks because you'd recognise his voice,' mused Jo. 'I think it's Professor Russell from the University.'

'The Egyptologist?'

'Yes, why, do you know him?'

'No I didn't get to arrange it.'

'Arrange what?'

'I'm a criminology student and I was following the Anubis investigation.'

'Yes, we saw that from your room.'

'I wanted more background on Egypt and Anubis, so my tutor approached Professor Russell, to ask if he'd give me some time and insights.'

'That's why you were taken then.'

'Probably. Oh, God! So he knew what I was doing. What if he does to me what he did to those other poor girls?'

'How do you mean?' Jo needed to know how much Lindsay knew of Anubis' unorthodox method of killing his victims.

'Well he killed them! Isn't that enough? Oh, God, what are we to do?' Lindsay's bravado cracked and she began crying.

Jo shuffled round and gave the young girl a hug. 'It'll be alright. Come on now, we can't let him think he's broken us. We must be brave. Alright?'

Lindsay nodded and sniffed back her tears.

'Is there anything at all you can tell me about him?'

'No, sorry and if I say too much or look at him too closely, I get zapped for my troubles.'

'Zapped? So that's what happened. What is he using do you think?'

'Looks like a cattle prod thingy to me. You know the ones they hit the poor cows with to disorientate them before they're for the chop.'

Jo didn't like the images that piece of information evoked and she wondered how many shocks her body could take before it started shutting down. She didn't think it would be that many. She had to get out.

'Lindsay, do you know where we are?'

'No, not really. All I know is that there is this little room and then the open area outside, where he has some sort of metal table that he's tied me up to.'

'Have you seen any way out of there?'

Lindsay nodded. 'Well there are wooden steps going upwards, but I don't remember being brought down them.'

'Any windows?'

'No, none.'

'That goes with what I know,' said Jo. 'I think we're in an abandoned house, near Bosham. As you say there are steps upstairs, my guess is that we're in the basement and the door is at the top of those stairs. We need for one of us to get away. Are you up for that?'

'Definitely, what do you want me to do?'

'When he comes to get one or the other of us, I'll barrel into him. Hopefully I'll take him by surprise, and I want you to be behind me so you can immediately run past him and bolt for the stairs.'

'What if the door at the top is locked?'

'That's a chance we'll have to take. Hopefully my appearance will have surprised and worried him. We'll just have to hope that because of that he might make mistakes.'

'Are you sure?'

Jo felt she had to be honest with Lindsay.

'No, but it's the best chance we're going to get. Once you get out, run away as fast as you can, flag down a car and tell the driver to ring the police and tell them you have an urgent message for DS Eddie Byrd from DI Jo Wolfe. Have you got that?'

Lindsay repeated, 'DS Eddie Byrd and DI Jo Wolfe.'

'That's right. Tell him what's happened and who you are, he'll come and get me out and call an ambulance for you.'

Lindsay nodded.

Jo watched her in the gloom. 'It'll work Lindsay. But you need to be positive and brave. There will be no room for hesitation. We must take him by surprise. It won't work twice, so we must get it right first time. OK?'

Lindsay nodded.

Jo smiled and tried not to show her own worries about the flimsiest of plans.

Jo had gleaned from Lindsay that she had heard Anubis rattling keys just before the door opened. It also opened outwards which Jo could use to her advantage. They agreed that as soon as they heard the jingling of keys, they would be ready. Jo would stand where the lock on the door was, ready for it to open and Lindsay would be right behind her.

All they could do now was wait.

# 47

The two women had relaxed somewhat and were sitting by the door on the floor, when they heard the faint jangle of keys.

'That's him,' hissed Lindsay.

'Right.'

Jo leapt up. She was tired and thirsty but pushed aside those needs to concentrate on getting Lindsay out.

Everything felt as though it were happening in slow motion. The key was placed into the lock. It was turned. The tumblers fell into place. The door opened a crack… and Jo pounced. She put her shoulder into a rugby tackle, pushing herself off with her feet and drove into Anubis with everything she had. All her fear and frustration was poured into the task and she barrelled into Anubis taking him by surprise.

'Run!' she shouted to Lindsay and felt the girl push past her and bolt for the stairs. Anubis must have stumbled backwards, away from the door, as it swung wide open. As Jo suddenly had nothing to push up against, she stumbled and cried out as Anubis got hold of her clothes and pulled her towards him.

The next thing she felt was a bolt of pain, which firstly ran up her arm, then her neck and caused stars to burst in front of her eyes. She fell to the floor, limbs jerking, all control of her body suddenly gone.

The fog in Jo's brain slowly lifted and her sight started to return. But there was something wrong with her body. She couldn't lift her arms or her hands, nor her legs and feet. Raising her head to find out what the problem was, she realised she couldn't do that either. Her head was fixed, staring at the ceiling. She was cold, not just with shock, but because she was naked. As a huge wolf's head loomed over her, she began to scream, until a rag was stuffed into her mouth. That shut her up.

'Ah, Detective Inspector, you're back with us. I hope I didn't hurt you. Well actually that's a lie, I really hope I did.'

His laugh was evil and maniacal and made Jo shiver even more. Shock was starting to set in, and her eyes bulged, and cheeks puffed out as she tried to swear at him.

'Shall I take this out?' he asked. 'Will you behave if I do? Not that anyone will hear your screams. We're far too isolated for that. But because it becomes tiresome. I can't be doing with the noise. So, shall I take it out?'

Jo mumbled, 'Yes please.' Which bore no resemblance whatsoever to the words she was trying to articulate.

Anubis leaned over her again and began to pull the rag out of her mouth. Jo spat and spluttered as the last of it cleared her dry mouth.

'That was a very brave stunt you pulled earlier,' he said to her. 'I must confess to being taken by surprise.'

'You're finished, Professor,' Jo croaked. 'Lindsay

will bring help.'

'Sure of that, are you? How do you know she got away? For all you know she could be back in the locked room.'

Jo knew what he was doing but refused to be rattled. He was trying to undermine her confidence and belief that Lindsay would have managed to get away and run for help.

'She will have got away and raised the alarm,' insisted Jo. 'If she didn't get away, prove it to me! Go on, get her out and show her to me.'

'Oh, shut up will you. I'll do no such thing. In case you hadn't noticed I'm rather busy, and I'm the one in charge, not you anymore. So if you'll excuse me, I have preparations to make,' and he stuffed the gag back into Jo's mouth, then moved out of her line of sight.

As she heard him clattering around, Jo tried to stay positive. She needed Lindsay to have gotten away so she could be found. But what if Lindsay didn't get away? Well, then they were both doomed to die.

Jo knew the Professor wouldn't take the chance of leaving either of them alive.

Her thoughts strayed to the maniacal way he'd laughed earlier. She felt she could see something behind those glass eyes of the wolf's head. Something glinting, something biding its time, just waiting for the right time to pounce. The thought sent yet another shiver through her, but this time it had nothing to do with being cold and everything to do with being scared shitless.

# 48

Mick Wolfe's stomach rumbled, causing him to check his watch. Where on earth was Jo? She was very late with the Chinese take-away. Something must have happened at work and she'd been delayed. Grabbing his mobile he called Jo, yet again, but the call just rang out. Which was strange. Jo always answered his calls to her, even when she was busy at work.

With small prickles of worry lifting the hairs on his arms, Mick rang Byrd.

'Oh hi, Eddie, Mick Wolf here,' he said as Eddie Byrd answered the call.

'Hi, Mick, what can I do for you?'

'I was just wondering if you knew what had delayed Jo. She was calling for a takeaway on the way home, but she's not arrived.'

'I don't know, Mick. Have you rung her?'

Mick tried very hard not to sigh in frustration. 'Of course I have, Eddie,' he said carefully, not wanting to rub Eddie up the wrong way. 'But she's not picking up and I expected her home an hour ago. So I thought she might still be at work with you.'

Mick realised he was very much hoping that was

the case, but it was becoming increasingly clear it wasn't.

'No, sorry, Mick, I left work, oh nearly two hours ago now, I guess. She seemed fine then.'

'Shit. This isn't like her, Eddie.'

'No, you're right. She was gathering up her stuff to leave when I did. If something had happened with the case, she'd have called me back.'

'And called me to explain and cancel supper.'

'Let me ring the nick and I'll call you back.'

The line went dead and Mick tried Jo's mobile again, but she still didn't answer.

Becoming very concerned now, Mick started to pace and didn't stop until Byrd rang him back.

'Mick, I've talked to the desk sergeant. Jo left a few minutes behind me. He saw her climb into her car and drive away on the CCTV screen. There didn't seem to be anything wrong. I've no idea what's going on, but I don't like it.'

'Neither do I, Byrd.'

'Leave it with me, I'll put a call out to all the traffic cars to be on the alert for Jo's car. In the meantime I'll get CCTV to try and track her movements and go back through the ANPR records. What take-away would she be going to? Let's see if she made it there.'

Mick gave Eddie the information he wanted. 'Sung Lee Chinese takeaway just off the A27. It's a bit of a hidden gem, great food at great prices.'

Mick shut up, realising he was gabbling on.

'Thanks, Mick, I'll keep you posted. And you'll ring me if you hear from Jo?'

'Of course, Eddie. Thanks for your help. I hope we're not over reacting.'

'No we definitely aren't. If the Boss is in trouble, we need to find her. And fast.'

# 49

The longer Jo was strapped to the table, the more she thought that Lindsay must have got away. If not, surely the girl would have found a way to let Jo know she was still alive. Banging on the door of their cell-like room. Screaming. Shouting. Anything.

Jo closed her eyes and prayed.

*PLEASE let Byrd find me. Please HELP him and the team. They WILL find Anubis. They WILL find me. They WILL have found Lindsay. Someone WILL have heard her story and alerted the police. Please let Byrd find me. Please help him and the team...*

Jo kept up her silent mantra as tears leaked out of her closed eyelids. But she had to force herself to remain optimistic. Otherwise she'd give up. And Jo Wolfe didn't do giving up. She'd never given up after her accident. She'd never given up when she'd realised she had a brand-new gift as a result. As awful as that gift was, as scary as the visions were, she'd never given up hope that she would find the victims, or the perpetrators of the most horrible crimes.

Ergo she couldn't give up hope now. She had to believe that she'd see Byrd again. The night they'd spent together had been special. Even though she'd vowed it would never happen again, she hadn't meant it. Not really. She wanted one more night with him. One more night when she wouldn't feel so alone. One more night when the presence of a warm body beside her would keep the nightmares at bay. One more chance at…

She felt the air change on her face and opened her eyes. Goosebumps pimpled her skin, crawling down her arms and legs. The cave was thick with the stench of death. The wolf's head loomed over her. It was so very intimidating, as she was sure it was meant to be. But this time it seemed real. Seemed as though the Professor and Anubis were as one, and that the wolf's head was no longer a disguise. She watched as the creature's jaws yawned open, saliva dripping from its fangs onto her skin. The drops stung her flesh. It was as though she was being burned with acid. Then the apparition spoke.

'Oh good, I'm glad you're awake for this,' he said. 'One of the preparations for the ritual is your hair.' The Professor's voice had deepened. It rumbled through the cave and Jo could feel the metal table vibrating.

Anubis held up a large pair of scissors for her to see.

Jo realised he was about to cut her hair. But not if she could help it. She tried to move her head, but of course she couldn't. Nor her arms, nor her legs. She wouldn't be able to stop him.

He grabbed the combs that were still in place on the top of her head and released her black hair. It was shoulder length, but Jo rarely wore it down, preferring to tie it up out of the way, especially when at work.

Anubis laughed. 'I'm afraid I'm not a hairdresser and there isn't much room, what with your head being pinned down and all, but I'll do my best.'

She felt Anubis grab handfuls of her hair and could hear the sawing noise as the scissors cut it. She imagined he was fashioning it to give her the blunt Egyptian style. He leaned over her face and Jo could feel the scissors cut across her forehead. Jesus, he was even giving her a fringe.

She was so bloody cross. How dare he violate her like this. Make her into an image that pleased him. If she got away – no WHEN she got away – she'd have to have a short haircut, as soon as possible. No way was she leaving it the way he'd cut it.

'There, that's much better. Would you like to see?'

If Jo hadn't a gag in her mouth, she would have told him to go and fuck himself. But unfortunately that wasn't an option.

Anubis unbuckled the strap holding her head and held up a small hand mirror. She didn't want to look and closed her eyes, refusing to open them.

He slapped her face.

She still wouldn't look in the mirror.

'Open your eyes, bitch!' he shouted, and Jo was once more subjected to saliva dropping from his fangs. Anubis clearly wasn't used to being defied. After slapping her this way and that, Jo still refused to look in the mirror. He finally gave up.

'Oh well, your loss. I've still got things to do, so as much as I'd like to indulge you, I really must press on.'

Anubis turned away from her and Jo heard tinkling behind her head and wondered if he was setting up the scales to weigh her heart. The thought made her scream, but it was too muffled through the gag. Still she got another slap in the face for her trouble, so she decided to stop. To save her strength. She turned back to her mantras.

*My team WILL find you. They WILL find me. They WILL find Lindsay. My team WILL find me. They*

*WILL find Lindsay...*

But she was becoming desperate. She had no idea who she was dealing with. It no longer seemed to be the Professor with a mask on his head. Instead, she had been confronted with a beast, who emanated pure evil.

# 50

Shirley Jones and her husband Tony were coming back from a trip to the cinema. Bowling along the road in their non-descript Ford, they discussed the film.

'To be honest,' said Tony, 'I thought it was a load of rubbish!'

'No, it wasn't that bad, surely.'

'Oh come off it, zombies are so yesterday.'

Shirley laughed. 'So yesterday – where on earth did you get that phrase from?'

'One of the kids at school. It's my way of staying up to date. Being hip, innit?'

That made Shirley laugh even harder. 'Tony, you're a primary school teacher. The last thing we both are is – what the hell?'

'Sorry?'

'Stop! There's a girl in the road!'

Shirley couldn't believe her eyes. Caught in their headlights was a young woman. At least Shirley thought it was a young woman. She had short, bobbed hair that was a wild halo around her head. She appeared to be dressed in a cotton shift that was filthy and wasn't that blood on it?

Tony brought the car to a halt. 'Jesus. Is she okay? She looks like a character from the film we've just seen. If anyone looks like a zombie, it's her.'

'I don't think she's okay at all. Neither do I think she's an extra in a cult horror movie.'

At that point the woman collapsed. She did a slow-motion gracious pirouette, ending up face down on the road.

'Tony, call an ambulance,' Shirley shouted as she opened the car door.

'Where are you going?'

'To help her, of course. Now phone the bloody ambulance.'

Shirley leapt out of the car and ran to the woman, who appeared to be unconscious. She manipulated her the best she could into the recovery position, then took off her coat and covered the young woman with it. She really wanted to move her into the car to keep her warm but was afraid to in case she had injuries that couldn't be seen. She took off her cardigan and bundled it up to place under her head. As she did, the woman started to mumble.

'Help, got to help her.'

'Help who?' Shirley leaned down, putting her ear near to the woman's mouth.

'The policewoman. I've got to tell Byrd. Wolfe is in the empty house.'

'Bird? What are you talking about? Birds?'

'No, policeman called Byrd. Got to tell him where she is. Please help. It's very important.'

The woman stopped talking and she began crying.

'Help is coming, don't worry,' Shirley said and held the girl's hand tightly. 'I can hear the sirens. It's going to be okay.'

A few minutes later the ambulance pulled up on the empty road in front of them and a doctor and a medic emerged from the back doors. Then a police car stopped behind them, and another in front of the ambulance. Their lights continued to flash as two uniformed officers began to put cones out protecting them from any vehicles that may come along. Not that Shirley thought that likely as the parts of Chichester around Bosham were sparsely populated.

As the doctor started his examination, the medic turned to Shirley.

'Do you know what happened? Has she said anything?'

'We just found her in the middle of the road. She collapsed onto the tarmac, so my husband called for you lot. I covered her the best I could to keep her warm.'

'Thank you, I'm sure that's helped a lot. Has she said anything about where she's come from?'

'She was mumbling about something. Birds and wolves and policemen.'

'I'm sorry?'

'She kept saying to get help. To tell Bird where she is. Where Wolf is, I think. She was most insistent and very upset. Does it make any sense to you?'

But the medic didn't answer the question. 'We'll be off soon, as we need to get her to the hospital. The paramedic turned his attention to the woman as she heard the doctor say, 'Let's get her on a stretcher and inside as quickly as we can. Her body's shutting down.'

The medic nodded his agreement and disappeared into the ambulance.

By this time the police had finished securing the site and approached the couple, guiding them onto the grass verge. 'Good evening. Could you tell us what happened please?'

Once again Shirley told the officers what had

happened, with Tony chipping in what he thought were salient details, only to be thrown a look by Shirley. One that said shut up you don't know what you're talking about – let me handle this, making him look at the floor and kick the grass. Once again, she told them about the woman's pleas to tell the police about birds and wolves and heads.

'I'm sorry?'

'She kept saying to get help. To tell Bird where she is. Where Wolf is, I think. She was most insistent and very upset. Does it make any sense to you?'

The two officers glanced at each other, a look passing between them that Shirley didn't understand. 'Are you sure you've remembered that correctly, madam? It's very important,' said one of them. 'Can you try and recall her exact words?'

Shirley bit her lip as she thought back. 'A policeman called Bird. Got to tell him where she is. Please help. It's very important.'

One of the officers moved away and began talking into the radio on his shoulder. Shirley heard a snipped, 'Control, patch me through to D S Byrd. It's urgent.'

'Thank you for your help, madam,' said the one who'd stayed behind. 'Can you give me your contact details please?'

Once they'd done that, the officers said that they could leave, and they'd be in touch if they needed any further information. Shirley wasn't at all sure what further information she could give but nodded all the same. As they climbed back into their vehicle, both police cars stayed where they were, lights still flashing. Waiting. For what, Shirley didn't know.

# 51

Anubis was still clattering away near to Jo. She was amazed that he had so much to do. He seemed to be lifting items and chanting incantations. Then something touched her chest. He'd laid something on her. It was cold and nicked her skin as he put it down.

The images exploded in her brain. Whatever it was that he'd placed on her chest had been used on his other victims.

*It was like being in the middle of a nightmare that had no end. Jo heard high pitched screams that hurt her ears and she saw snatched pictures of girls with black, short bobbed hair. She saw the three victims, Alison, Charlie and Imogen, but there were others. Lots of them, their faces flickering and fading in and out like a gory slideshow. Blood, dark hair, white faces. Faster and faster the images went, chilling her already cold body, overwhelming her with their pleas for help that Jo couldn't provide.*

And then it was over. It was all so hopeless and Jo felt helpless, trapped in Anubis' lair, destined to become one of his victims herself. Tears streamed down the sides of her head and pooled on the table.

# 52

Byrd couldn't remember when he'd last felt this tired. He'd just had a shower and was trying to relax when Mick Wolfe had phoned him, looking for Jo. The case was getting to all of them, but he was worried about Jo. She was in danger of burning out. He was sure of it. And where in the hell was she now? The bloody woman didn't half get on his nerves.

But she was DI Wolfe. Eddie had to remember that. She was not just his friend. She was his superior officer. His partner. They were used to spending all day every day in each other's company. He didn't want to lose that rapport. Would it be worth it for sex?

But deep down he knew what had happened between them was far more than just sex and he was sure Jo had felt it as well. Even though they'd both said they hadn't. Agreed with each other. Neither brave enough to reveal how they felt.

He was just drifting off to sleep in his chair as he waited for news, when his mobile rang. Then his landline. Then his Facebook messenger app trilled. Bloody hell someone wanted him urgently. Maybe they'd located Jo? He answered his mobile.

'DS Byrd.'

'Oh, thank god I've found you, sir,' the voice said. 'Constable Riley here. I'm on the coast road near Bosham.'

'Yes?' Byrd was rapidly coming awake.

'A young girl was found wandering on the road. She's been taken to the general hospital, but she said she had a message for a policeman named Byrd from a wolf. So I figured that could be you.'

Prickles of fear began running up and down Byrd's spine.

'What's the matter with DI Wolfe? Did she say?'

'Just that she'd got to tell you where she is. I took it to mean DI Wolfe. What do you think?'

'I think that could be right and that I need to try and find Jo. Are you still on the road?'

'Yes, sir, there are two cars here and a total of four officers.'

'Very well, one pair should stay on the road and secure the scene where the girl was found. The other two should have a poke around in the immediate area. I'll send forensics to help.'

'Are you coming?' the officer wanted to know.

'Yes, but I'm going to the hospital first. I need to try and find out where the girl has come from and talking to her would be the quickest way to find out. I hope.'

'If she's able to talk.'

'Exactly. I'm leaving home in a minute. Keep me up to date on my mobile.'

'Yes, sir.'

Byrd grabbed his keys and badge off the kitchen worktop. He ran to the car and once the Bluetooth was activated, he said, 'Call Jo.'

When there was still no reply from Jo's mobile, he changed tack and said, 'Call Wolfe.' He needed to speak to Jo's father. He wasn't sure it would make Mick feel any better, but he had a duty to know. He was an ex-police officer and because of that, he deserved Byrd's respect.

# 53

At the hospital Byrd rushed through to A&E. Ignoring the reception desk, he pushed through the doors marked 'Do Not Enter'. He'd been there often enough to know the layout in detail. Lindsay would be in a cubicle by now, he just had to find the right one.

A nurse stepped into his path. 'Can I help you? You're not allowed back here.'

'Yes I am,' said Byrd, flashing his warrant card as he didn't recognise the nurse who had stopped him. 'A young girl was found on a country road up by Bosham. Where is she?'

'Being worked on by the doctor. You'll have to wait outside.'

'No, sorry, not going to happen. Which cubicle is she in?'

'Please leave...'

Byrd interrupted her. 'You're not listening to me. This is a matter of life and death. This girl knows the whereabouts of DI Wolfe who is missing, so you are going to let me see her NOW!'

Eddie knew he shouldn't lose his temper but couldn't help it. He wasn't going to be stopped now, and especially not by a nurse who had ideas above her station. He saw a doctor's head poke out of a cubicle along to the left. 'Byrd is that you?'

Eddie had never been so glad to see a friendly face. It was a stroke of luck that one of his best friends was on duty. He stalked past the now embarrassed nurse as Gill emerged from the curtain. 'Is it this girl you're interested in?'

'The one found on the road near Bosham?'

'That's her. Come in.'

As Byrd followed him in, Gill said, 'Do you recognise her?'

'Bloody right I do. She's our missing girl. We were afraid she was the latest victim in the serial killer case we're working on.'

'I think she was, but she managed to get away. She keeps saying she must tell Byrd where Wolfe is. I was going to ring you, but you beat me to it.'

Byrd leaned over the bed and stroked Lindsay's face. 'Hello, Lindsay, can you hear me?'

The girl's eyelids fluttered.

'She's going to be very sleepy. We've given her a sedative. She's got some nasty burns on her which we've treated. But we don't think she's got any broken bones. She'll be going for a scan soon which will give us a better picture.'

'Lindsay,' said Byrd. 'Where have you been? Can you remember?'

'Empty house near the water,' she mumbled. 'Wolf. Bird. Got to let him know. Big bad wolf! No! No! Leave me alone!' Lindsay tried to push herself up off the pillow.

'It's okay, Lindsay, I'm Byrd. You've let me know. Get some rest now. Come on, lie back. Let the doctors help you.'

A faint nod and then Lindsay relaxed.

'Is that useful?' Gill asked.

'Very. Thanks, mate,' and Byrd left the cubicle.

'Hey,' Gill called after him. 'Don't be a stranger!'

Byrd raised his arm in reply but didn't stop. He needed to raise the rest of the team and to work out where the hell Jo might be.

The next phone call made that task slightly easier.

'DS Byrd? We've located DI Wolfe's car.'

# 54

Waiting for key members of the team to arrive at the station felt like hours to Byrd, but, was only about 15 minutes. But those 15 minutes could be crucial Byrd knew. Where was Jo? Was she still alive? Would they be too late? These thoughts were eating Byrd up and he had to stop it otherwise he'd never be able to look at the operation with an objective eye. By the time Judith, Bill and Jill had arrived, he'd a large-scale map of the area around Bosham laid out.

'So where do you think she could be, Boss?' asked Jill.

'At the moment I've no idea. And that's the trouble. We could waste valuable time checking out the whole area and being in totally the wrong place.'

'There's a way to narrow it down,' said Judith, her analytical mind coming to the fore.

'Go for it,' said Byrd as Judith grabbed a marker pen.

'Right, where was her car found?'

Eddie pointed to it. 'Here, if that is where she left it and it hasn't been moved to a completely different location by Anubis.'

Judith ignored his scepticism and marked it on the map. 'So we search around this area, say half a mile circumference. What do you think?'

Byrd peered at the map. In the target area was an abandoned house they'd seen before. It was near to where the girls had been washed up on the edge of Bosham. Could they have missed something? He made a snap decision and started issuing orders to Judith.

'Brief the Commander. Get him to send a tactical team to meet us where Jo's car is. We'll also need uniform boots on the ground to conduct a close search of the entire area. You stay here and act as the central hub for information and operations.'

Judith nodded and moved away to her desk as Eddie, Bill and Jill gathered up their stuff and ran for their cars.

With blue's and two's going, the two cars raced out of the station car park and into the night.

# 55

Byrd only had to wait 10 minutes by Jo's car before the tactical team arrived. The occupants streamed out of their van, each dressed in black clothing, brandishing a semi-automatic rifle. Their leader approached Eddie, with his hand held out.

'DS Byrd? I'm Inspector Tony Small.'

Once the two men had shaken hands, Tony said, 'So can you brief us please. We understand your DI is being held somewhere in these marshlands.'

'Yes, we believe she is somewhere in a half mile radius of here.'

'Very well, I'll split up the men into teams of two and send them out covering north, south, east and west.'

'Do you have a set of night vision goggles I could use?'

'Yeah, sure,' and Tony disappeared into the van. Within moments he'd returned, the goggles in his hand. 'And you want these because?'

'So I can see what's happening as you and your team search the area.'

'Are you sure? You're not planning to search for

your DI yourself?'

'Heavens, no. More than my job's worth.'

'Okay, glad to hear it. Stay here and I'll report in on a regular basis.'

'Thanks,' Eddie said and moved away before Tony Small saw the subterfuge written on his face. He was glad the darkness helped cover it, as Eddie had no intention of staying where he was.


Bryd, Bill and Jill moved as quietly as they could through the undergrowth in the direction of the abandoned house they'd checked weeks before.

They stopped once the house came into view. 'We don't know if this is the correct house, Byrd,' Bill whispered. 'Can you see anything through the goggles?'

'No, not a damn thing. I guess I needed something that would record the heat source. Let's go around the back of the house.'

Byrd led his little band around the house, but there was no sign of life. They couldn't see anyone. Or hear anyone.

'There don't seem to be any cameras,' Bill noticed. 'What do you reckon we should do?' he asked Byrd.

'We have to be really careful and really sure. This is the Guv we're talking about. We mustn't go in based on emotions but on solid evidence. Alright?'

'Right, Boss,' said Jill. 'So what are we doing?

'Going in of course,' said Byrd.

# 56

They drew a blank. There was no one in the house. No Anubis and no Jo. Byrd tried to be upbeat but was inconsolable. He was convinced that when they found her, she would be dead.

He said, 'He isn't here. I was so sure we'd find him here. Where can he have gone? It's like he's gone down a rabbit hole.'

'Yeah,' said Jill. 'Or a tunnel, you know like they had in the days of smugglers. They had tunnels from their house to a cave on the beach where the boats would land, that sort of thing.'

'You a history buff or what?' asked Bill.

'Yeah guess so, I like reading about things like that.'

'Okay so where would the entrance to a hidden tunnel be in a house,' asked Byrd.

'Well from the basement. But there isn't one.'

'You sure about that? Tunnels and smugglers?'

'Not 100 per cent, but it's got to be worth a go, Boss, hasn't it?'

Byrd thought for a moment. 'Okay let's check in all the ground floor rooms again.'

Despite an extensive search, there was nothing. Nothing on the walls, nor on the floor.

'Maybe there's a door,' said Jill, ever the optimist.

'Where the fuck would there be a door? This is a bloody wild goose chase and all the time the Guv is missing. How is this helping exactly?'

'Byrd, there's a pantry here, in the kitchen,' called Bill.

'So?' Byrd was becoming depressed and had trouble feigning interest.

'So why aren't there any shelves on the back wall?' said Bill.

'Sorry?'

'Well if you have a pantry that goes nowhere, you cover every wall with shelves, for maximum storage, yes?'

'Suppose so, sorry I'm not a kitchen designer.'

But Jill was examining the wall.

'What are you doing?' snapped Byrd.

'Trying to find a catch if it's a door. Could be one of those push ones, you know? Push the door in the right place and it opens up.'

'Out of the way,' said Byrd.

'What?'

'Out of the bloody way!'

Byrd grabbed an old rusted piece of metal off the floor and stabbed at the wall.

The metal bar went straight through.

It was a false wall.

Which meant there was something behind it.

# 57

Jo had been waiting for something to happen to her. She was still strapped to the table, still with the scalpel on her chest, still not sure if Lindsay had managed to get away. Then Anubis turned and leered at her.

'It's time to get you ready,' he said. Jo realised from the guttural tones that Anubis was still in charge. She wondered if the Professor was in there somewhere. She wondered if she could appeal to that person. The human being behind the mask. Behind the ogre.

'There's no need for this, you know…' she began.

That made Anubis laugh, a brittle sound with no humour behind it.

'You can stop and give yourself up.'

'Oh, Jo, have you forgotten that you're the one strapped naked to a table? You arrest me! That's priceless, it really is.' He threw back his wolf's head and howled with laughter. It made Jo think of wolves howling at the moon and a shiver ran over her.

But she was determined not to be bowed by him. 'Not me, my colleagues. They'll be on their way by now. You haven't got much longer.'

'I've got plenty of time, thanks all the same. No one will ever find us here.'

'Byrd will. He'll come for me.'

'Ha! So that's your hope is it? Lover boy will come, will he? Trust me, you're going to be sorely disappointed, my dear. No one is coming. The day of reckoning is upon you. It's your destiny. And I shall enjoy sending you to ROT IN HELL FOR ALL TIME!'

Jo could hear the excitement in his voice. He moved to the end of the table, by her feet. At his touch she wanted to scream, but she refused to give him the satisfaction and swallowed it back, ending up with a grimace on her face and a choking noise in her throat.

'Ah, so you're determined not to scream, are you? Well we'll see how long that lasts.'

Then something cold hit her right foot, a squelching noise followed it and Jo realised her foot was being wrapped in something wet and sticky. Then he turned to the left foot.

'The bandages kept coming off the other girls,' he said in a conversational tone. 'So this time I'm sticking them on. I wanted to use the bandages they use in hospitals to put plaster casts on, but I needed warm water, which I just haven't got. So I've had to make do with wallpaper paste. It should do the trick.'

The gloopy mess was cold and made her shiver.

'I really wanted to wrap your legs together, but I decided undoing the straps wouldn't be a good idea.

The bandages were up to her knees.

Then travelling up her thighs.

The nearer he got to the top of her legs the more she started to hyper ventilate. She knew what would come after the bandages and as he moved up her hips, she began to scream.

She was given a blast with Anubis' cattle prod.

'Shut up,' he hissed in her ear, his fetid breath making her want to vomit. But she did as she was told.

Anubis cocked his head as if to hear better. 'There's someone upstairs,' he said.

'I told you...' but Jo's retort was silenced with another prod.

'How dare they! What right have they to come into my lair!' Anubis reared up and the roar that followed was the most horrible sound Jo had ever heard.

'How many will there be?' he shouted at Jo.

'I, um, I.'

'HOW MANY?' he screamed.

'Tactical,' Jo said, hoping to God that's who was outside. 'Armed officers, AK47's. They'll shoot first and ask questions later.' Which was a blatant lie but seemed to help her situation.

'I don't want to die!' The voice didn't belong to Anubis. It was thin and reedy.

'Professor?' said Jo. 'Is that you? Are you in there?'

But the only response Jo got was another roar from Anubis.

Suddenly it was as if the air in the basement began to spin. Jo felt wind rushing around the confined space. She was buffeted this way and then that by it and she would have been lifted from the table if she hadn't been tied down. Her hair was blown over her face, but through the strands she saw Anubis rise into the air. Riding on the maelstrom. As if in the eye of a tornado. Scalpels and other instruments rose into the air and spun around him.

Jo was sure she could hear the Professor screaming but was powerless to help. She could only hope her bindings stayed intact, otherwise she would be torn from the table and whipped around the room as well.

The noise of the wind increased to a fever pitch and

Jo wondered if she'd be able to hear again.

'I will return, and you will ALL DIE!' Anubis shouted and deep inside her Jo felt the vibrations from the deep throated scream.

Then he turned and fled.

# 58

They all heard it. The scream. And then the roar. Never had Byrd heard such awful sounds. Jo was being tortured. He had to get to her!

Only movement would chase away the terror of what he imagined was happening to Jo. She could be being cut open while they were waiting on the opposite side of this bloody stupid door. Spurred into action, Byrd slammed his shoulder into the wall which started to disintegrate. A few more well-placed blows and there was an opening big enough to clamber through.

He wanted to rush through the opening, but his training kicked in. Forcing himself to be cautious, he clicked on his mobile phone to light up what was beyond the door. He was immediately glad he'd showed restraint, for on the other side was a set of steps. They'd found the basement.

Not knowing what they would find at the bottom, Byrd gestured for the others to keep quiet and one by one the little group made their way down the stairs, hugging the wall. Each slow step was torture but was nothing compared with what Jo might be going through. They had no idea if Anubis was still there, or if he'd fled. But if so, where had he gone? How would he get away? Byrd's mind whirred round and round, his breath coming in short bursts and his shirt was damp with sweat, chilling him and causing him to shiver.

What they saw at the bottom made Byrd stagger backwards and bump into Bill.

'Jesus,' whispered Bill peering over Eddie's shoulder. 'Is that the Boss?'

Byrd could only nod and stare transfixed. He didn't trust himself to speak. Strapped to a metal table, with legs and part of the torso wrapped in bandages, was what looked as though it could be a woman with short dark hair. But was she alive, or dead?

'Jo? Is that you?' he croaked.

'Byrd,' came the whisper. 'You came.'

The relief at finding the DI alive brought tears to his eyes that he dashed away before rushing to the table. 'You okay, Boss?'

He touched her hand and tried hard not to look at Jo's exposed breasts. A memory flittered through his addled brain of their one and only night together, which was an entirely inappropriate thought.

'He's gone, Byrd,' she said. 'We heard you coming, and he ran off.'

'Where, Jo? Where did he go?'

'That way, deeper into the basement, there must be a tunnel as he's not come back!'

'Ok, rest now. Bill's got some water for you.'

She nodded her head. 'Go, Byrd. Find him,' she pleaded and with a final touch of her face, Byrd turned and ran off into the gloom.

# 59

The way through the tunnel was lit by dim bulbs strung along the ceiling, Byrd had nearly tripped over the source of the electricity used to power them – three car batteries. He just hoped they'd last before he reached the end, wherever that might be. As the sounds of Bill, Jill and Jo in the basement faded away, somewhere in the distance he could hear the steady drip, drip of water, reminding him he was near to the water, on the edge of Bosham.

Byrd's mind kept flicking back to the image of Jo. Hurt, vulnerable, shocked. He'd do all he could to catch the bastard who did this to her. Of course, he would do that for any victim. But Jo? Well he had to admit how special she was. All this time he was hurrying towards the end of the tunnel, going as fast as he could in the dim light and on the stony ground that his feet constantly tripped against.

Suddenly losing his footing, he sprawled along the floor, grazing his hands and knees. Swearing roundly and loudly he forced himself up onto his knees, groaning as the gravel pitting them dug into his skin. He scrambled to his feet, pushing himself forward, he wasn't going to lose the bastard. He suddenly realised that he didn't know the identity of the man he was chasing. He'd forgotten to ask Jo if she knew who Anubis was.

Jo groaned as Jill and Bill helped her to swing her legs off the metal table and sit up on the edge of it. She was still swathed in bandages from the waist downwards, but Bill had cut the restraints around her ankles and wrists. He was in the process of tying plastic bags over her hands and feet and had already collected the bindings for forensic examination.

'You can lie back down now, Jo,' he said, but she struggled against him.

'Where's Byrd?' Jo croaked, her throat feeling like it had been coated with sandpaper.

'He's gone after Anubis,' said Jill. 'Don't worry, he'll be fine. He'll catch the bastard, you'll see.'

'Professor,' Jo muttered.

'Sorry, Guv, come again?'

'Anubis, is the professor.' She swayed with the effort of speaking. But she had to know the answer to her next question. 'Lindsay?'

'She's safe in hospital, Guv. She did a great job of helping us find out where you were.'

Jo nodded, wondering what was wrong with her head. She kept getting flashes of light in her eyes, she could hear crackling and smelled a faint odour of burning.

Bill put a blue forensic hair covering on her head. Jo wanted to rip it off, untie the bags on her hand and feet and run after Byrd. But knew that would be reckless. She was in no physical shape to do any such thing. Plus, they needed the forensic evidence off her body. She had to be sensible and so she lay back down on the unyielding, cold table.

'That's the way, Boss,' Jill said. 'The ambulance will be here soon.'

Jo didn't want to go to hospital but nodded her acceptance. It was time to help the investigation with as much evidence as she could give them and then rest and recuperate. She closed her eyes and the basement faded as she slipped into sleep, finally accepting that she was safe.


Byrd knew he was near the end of the tunnel as he could hear the lapping of water and the distant mournful cry of seagulls, but it still took him by surprise as he rounded a corner and was thrust out of the tunnel and into a cove. He looked around and shivered in the cold night air. Where the hell was the bastard? He was unsure of where exactly he was, but Bosham was lit by a full moon shining in a cloudless sky. Out on the water he caught the glimpse of a light, which came and went as Byrd watched it. He became mesmerised, then realised what it was. He grabbed his mobile. He needed to scramble the coastguard. They had to stop that boat. They just had to. It must be Anubis' boat. He couldn't be allowed to get away. Otherwise, in the future, more girls could be a victim of his, and Byrd couldn't bear that. Anubis had to be caught.

Once his orders had been relayed to the Coastguard there was nothing more he could do there and so he returned to the basement via the tunnel, this time managing to stay upright.

He burst into the open basement area, looking around for Jo. 'Bill, where's Jo? Is she OK?' Even Byrd could hear the desperation in his voice, revealing his emotion. That someone else might recognise it for what it meant, was of no interest anymore. If it revealed how he felt about Jo, then so be it.

Bill gave him a sideways look, then said, 'She's fine, Byrd. She's been taken to Chichester General.'

'Oh, right good. Thanks.' Byrd looked around, feeling a little lost.

'So I guess there was a tunnel there after all?'

'What? Fucking hell, sorry Bill. Yes, it's not very long and you come out into a small cove. It seems Anubis had a boat there. I could just about make it out on the water. I've contacted the coastguard and now I guess I need to bring the operational commander up to date.'

'Look there's nothing you can do here, why don't you go upstairs, make your phone calls and then check on the Boss.'

'Right, you're right, I think I will,' and he turned to go after Jo.

# 60

Byrd was glad that it was about 2 o'clock in the morning and therefore there was no one around to see his appalling driving. He couldn't seem to keep his mind on the road. All he could see was the pitiful sight of Jo strapped to that awful metal table. A cold, unfeeling, unforgiving slab of metal. He wanted so much to protect her. To make sure something like that would never happen to her again. But even he had to admit that he wasn't superman. And there would always be killers and maniacs to find and stop. It was their job. Pure and simple. And neither one of them would want to give it up.

He parked his car in the car park and put a sign on the dashboard saying, 'Police on active investigation' in the windscreen. He'd no idea if it would stop him getting a parking ticket, but as he had no money or cards on him, there wasn't much he could do about buying a ticket.

Running from the carpark to the A&E reception he met a burley security man with his arms out, stopping him in his tracks. 'Whoa there. Where are you going in such a hurry?'

Byrd pull out his warrant card. 'DS Byrd, Chichester Police. I'm looking for DI Wolfe, brought in earlier by ambulance.'

Before the man could reply, or throw him out, Byrd saw Gill and called out to grab his attention. Acknowledging him Gill said, 'It's okay, Fred. He can come through.'

'Very well, Doctor,' said Fred with as much gravitas as he could muster and fixed Eddie with a stare that said, I've got your number so no funny business. The unspoken threat made Byrd smile, but he turned away before Fred could see it.

'Thanks, Gill, I'm looking for Jo. Sorry, DI Wolfe.'

Walking back into A&E Gill said, 'Jo is okay but she's suffering from shock and dehydration.'

'Can I see her?'

'Of course.'

'Where is she?' Byrd looked around but all the cubicles appeared to be empty.

'Oh, sorry, she's been taken up to the ward, General Ward 2. Tell them I said you could see Jo and you can stay with her for a bit if you want to.'

All Byrd could do was nod at the kindness of his friend. He opened his mouth, but nothing came out and his eyes filled with tears of relief. He had been so worried about her.

'I know, Byrd,' said Gill, gripping Byrd's shoulder. 'I know. Go on. Off you go. If you fancy a coffee later, come down to A&E, we've got a pretty fancy machine here. None of that vending machine rubbish.'

# 61

The shock hit Jo, not in the ambulance, but when she was wheeled up to a ward. The nurses were just getting her settled in bed when she started shaking. And couldn't stop. She felt hot and cold at the same time. She was incapable of speech, just able to fix a nurse with a silent stare and hope she got the message that she needed help.

'Now, now, Jo, it's alright,' she said stroking Jo's hair and making Jo turn her head to look at her. 'It's all over now. Your safe.'

Jo managed to briefly nod her head as she felt a nurse take her other hand and then something cold flooded into her vein. She looked questioningly at the nurse talking to her.

'Don't worry, just a bit of Valium to relax you. Doctor's orders.'

Jo nodded and managed a whispered, 'Thank you,' as the tremors subsided as if by magic, to be replaced by fluffy clouds that she rode on. Away from the memories. Away from the injuries. And away from the pain.

Until she felt another touch on her hand. She

yelped. Who was it? A nurse? Anubis? She was too scared to open her eyes.

So the relief was immense when she heard a voice say, 'It's alright, Jo, it's only me.'

'Byrd?' she whispered.

'Yes. I just wanted to make sure you're okay, and to let you know we've got Anubis. The coastguard picked him up.'

He grasped her hand. She heard a chair being pulled towards the bed and then he sat down on it. All without letting go of her.

'So, are you okay?'

She nodded. 'I am now. Seeing you. And hearing that news.'

'Me too.' He placed her hand in between his. 'Now rest. I'll be here. I'll watch over you.'

'Thank you,' Jo mouthed as tears tracked their way down her face. 'Thank you.'

Finally, she was able to sleep. She'd face whatever tomorrow brought with Byrd. Together they'd be a force to be reckoned with.

# 62

By late afternoon the following day, Jo was deemed well enough to go home, but was under strict instructions that she wasn't to go back to work. She needed time for both her body and mind to heal. She still found herself trembling with fear when she thought back to her ordeal. That was no way for a police officer to feel. She knew she'd be a liability if she returned to work too soon.

She was waiting, sat on her hospital bed, when Byrd arrived to take her home. The last time she'd seen him, earlier that morning, he was creased and crumpled from sleeping in the chair next to her bed all night. He looked a lot better now, clearly having had a shower and changed his clothes. Some of the worry lines etched on his face last night had dissipated. Her dad had offered to come and get her, but Jo said not to worry, Byrd had it sorted.

'Okay, Boss? Ready?'

Jo smiled, 'Yep I'm just dandy. I've got my paperwork, a collection of tablets and strict instructions to take it easy and to go and see my GP for any follow up I might decide I need.'

'Come on, then,' he said and helped her off the bed, walking to a wheelchair parked within touching distance.

'Byrd! You can't be serious?'

'Afraid so, Boss. No wheelchair, no discharge. Hospital rules, so don't shoot the messenger. Now get in it!'

'Bloody hell,' Jo grumbled, but did as he said, she wasn't about to jeopardise her discharge.

It was a very strange experience to be pushed around the hospital corridors that normally she would be charging down to see victims and take statements. She felt vulnerable in the chair, something she hated as it took her back to the injuries she'd sustained in the riding accident. She knew how disabled people must feel who were permanently in a chair. It was very unsettling.

At the main doors, Jo wanted to get out of the chair and walk to the car, but Byrd insisted on her waiting while he brought the car around. Settled in the passenger seat, she watched the world go by, not speaking. Everything looked so ordinary and innocent. The people of Chichester going about their business, unaware of the things she had seen. The evil that men do. But she was glad that most people didn't know about gifts like Jo's. That only a handful of people did.

So, was it a gift or a curse? As awful as it was, as horrible as the visions were, Jo was coming to terms with them.

At home she climbed out of the car before Byrd could rush around and help her. That independent streak again. But she was very unsteady on the gravel drive, stumbling and causing Byrd to catch her in his arms. He didn't let go for the rest of the day. He helped her up the stairs. He helped her undress. He helped her into bed. He kissed away the pain of the burns on her body and then lay down next to her, enfolding her in his arms.

As Jo drifted off to sleep, she wondered why she hadn't done this before. It was the best she'd felt in a long time. Safe. With hope for the future. But she was troubled that it was with Byrd that she'd found happiness. Perhaps it was because they were already close. She trusted him with her life – let's face it he'd just saved it. Could this be misplaced emotion? A case of gratitude?

But then she thought of him again and went all quivery. She felt his arms around her, strong and dependable. She turned around to face him and they started to kiss, tentatively at first, but then with growing passion.

Jo put a finger on his lips and drew back. 'Isn't this a bad idea, Byrd?'

He nodded. 'It's not the most sensible thing we've ever done, but I can't stop. Can you?'

'Yes. No. Maybe. Oh fuck it,' said Jo and took her finger from his face and began kissing him with a fervour to match his own.

Then she pulled away again. 'This could be really awkward at work.'

'On the other hand it could be really wonderful working so closely together.'

Jo nodded and guessed only time would tell, as she slipped into a deep, dreamless sleep.

# 63

A couple of weeks after the close of the Anubis case, the team decided to go out and have a celebratory meal. The chosen venue was a great little Italian in the town centre.

The Professor had been charged with three counts of murder, five counts of kidnap and two counts of GBH from the torture he had subjected Jo and Lindsay to. No longer the great Anubis, the Professor looked small and weak at his brief appearance before the Magistrates court, when his case was referred to the Crown Court for trial.

All he'd said during interviews was, 'He's gone. I can't feel him anymore. He's gone.'

Russell had refused to say any more and psychological reports had been requested and so he was detained in a secure hospital. The official thinking was schizophrenia, as he'd clearly heard voices and then acted on them.

Jo wasn't so sure. The professor was now the broken, shell of a man, and Jo wondered if he was beyond repair. She'd had the full-on Anubis experience, and the thought that this might be the professor on steroids, just didn't sit well with her.

'I'm inclined to believe that Professor Russell was a victim of demonic possession, you know,' she confided in her father.

'I guessed as much.'

'The wolf head was so real. The jaws worked. There was stinging, burning saliva. A disgusting smell. And his voice… it was the voice of something not from this world.'

Mick nodded his head. 'Whatever it was it's gone now though, hasn't it?'

'Oh yes, at interview Professor Russell is practically catatonic. The being, if that's what it was, has done great damage to Russell's mind and body.'

'And you? How are you?'

'Oh, I'm feeling a lot stronger,' she told him as they dismantled her case wall.

'Are you sure, Jo?'

'Yes, thanks, Dad. But I still have regrets that Anubis killed three girls before I could stop him.'

'You can't beat yourself up too much, Jo,' he said, putting photographs into a box. 'You saved Lindsay, and let's face it you didn't kill the other three, the Professor did. Don't start feeling that you killed them, that way leads to madness.'

'I know what you mean, but at the moment I can't seem to detach myself from the case. The emotional pull still seems to be great.'

Mick took the papers out of her hand. 'Here, sit down,' he said and they both sank onto the sofa. 'You have to learn to come to terms with these things, Jo. The word is that the force likes you for these big cases. I hear the plan is that they are going to let you keep your own team permanently and then you'll be set up and ready for when the next big one comes along.'

'Really, Dad?'

'Really. But when you're told, looked surprised, okay?'

Jo laughed, 'Okay, and thanks. You're the best!'

They cleared the rest of the wall and Jo went to get ready to meet the team. Glancing at her watch she realised she was running late and hurried to turn the shower on.

# 64

Hurrying through Chichester city centre, Jo saw the lights of the restaurant in the distance. She kept up a quick pace and soon arrived. She could see the team at a table in the window. They weren't eating yet, thank goodness. They must have waited for her.

Byrd saw her and raised his glass. Their eyes locked and she went what she would previously have described as going all girly. She smiled at him and raised her hand in return to his greeting. There was an empty chair opposite him, obviously for her. Judith, Bill, Jill and Jeremy were already there, so she was the only one missing.

The explosion took her by surprise.

The bang echoed off the shops and buildings.

Bouncing. Ear bursting. The loudest noise she'd ever heard.

First the front of the restaurant disintegrated in front of her eyes. Then it felt as if all the air had been sucked out of the immediate area.

She couldn't breathe or speak. Nor could she hear anything. It was as though she were in a vacuum. All Jo could do was open her mouth in shock. There were no words to describe how she felt about what had just happened.

Her team. Gone.

Byrd. Gone.

Gradually her hearing came back and she could hear the tinkling of glass as it fell around her. It landed in her hair and on her clothes, like lethal snow. It was everywhere. There was a cacophony of screams from car alarms. Then came the sirens of police, ambulances and fire engines.

The blast had blown her off her feet and she got up slowly. Her hands and knees were cut, but she ignored the pain and the blood. All she could see was the gaping hole that was the front of the restaurant.

Where her team had sat.

Where Byrd had been.

\*\*\*

To be continued...

Jo Wolfe psychic detective crime thriller
Book 2


DI Jo Wolfe has a secret. She can touch the dead and see how they died. But no one must know.

After a great result in their last case, DI Jo Wolfe and her team decide to celebrate with a meal in a popular Italian in central Chichester. As Jo approaches the restaurant the unthinkable happens – a bomb detonates inside, and she must witness the death of the diners.

In the aftermath, Jo finds out that the target was a local MP and she receives a warning from the group responsible. They intend to kill politicians, 'painting red the powers' homes with crimson gore.' They intend to rid the UK of corrupt and incompetent MPs.

Can Jo rise above her grief and stop the ultra-right-wing group in their tracks?

Will the visions from the dead help her?

Or will her communication with the dead, hamper the investigation?

This is the second in a new series following Jo

Wolfe, a detective who developed psychic abilities after a riding accident. The only person who knows about her gift (or curse depending upon your point of view) is her father and together they attempt to right the wrongs of the living, with the aid of the dead.

Wendy Cartmell is well known for her bestselling, chilling crime thrillers and Sgt Major Crane mysteries. Several of them have ghostly and psychic elements and wanting to develop these themes further, she decided it was time she wrote a supernatural suspense series.

Now available from AMAZON.

Printed in Great Britain
by Amazon